EYES ON YOU

A GHOST STORY

STEVEN JENKINS

EYES ON YOU: A GHOST STORY

Copyright © 2017 by Steven Jenkins

Published in Great Britain in 2017
by Different Cloud Publishing.

CONTENTS

"For Lissa."

FREE BOOKS

For a limited time, you can download FREE copies
of *Spine, Burn The Dead*, and *Rotten Bodies* -
The No.1 bestsellers from Steven Jenkins.

Just visit: www.steven-jenkins.com

PROLOGUE

My phone vibrates in my pocket. It's Mum again, no doubt wondering where the hell I slept last night, or whether I skipped school today. I should answer it, tell her that I'm fine, and that I'm on my way home, but it's too much effort.

The sun is glaring down so I shield my eyes with my hand, the other one holding onto my swirling stomach, praying that I don't puke up for a third time. Shouldn't have had that last swig of vodka.

Home is just up ahead, so I focus on our red front door in the distance, using the parked cars to keep me from toppling over. Mum's car is parked in the drive. Dad's isn't. *That's worrying.* Any other day and that wouldn't set off a single alarm bell, but after yesterday, after the shit-storm, God knows where he is.

No, no scratch that, it's obvious where the cheating bastard is—shacked up with that fucking whore!

Hobbling up our drive, I stop by the front door. I don't think I'm quite ready to face Mum, especially with the worst ecstasy comedown ever. I lean against the wall and close my eyes, contemplating whether or not to head back the way I came, try to sleep for a few more hours.

No, I can't. I can't put this off any longer.

I let out a sigh, rub my burning eyes, and then open the front door.

Mum is in the living room, sitting on the couch, staring at the TV in a daze. Her eyes are bloodshot, her cheeks red and puffy, and she has the phone in one hand, and a tissue in the other.

She sees me standing in the doorway. "You're home," she says with urgency. "I've been calling you all morning. Where've you been?"

I shrug my shoulders. "Out," I reply, cagily, my voice hoarse, my throat dry and sore.

Mum sniffs loudly and wipes her nose with the tissue. "Sit down, Matt."

"Where's Dad?" I ask, as if I don't already know.

Mum doesn't answer. *I was right—he's with that fucking bitch again.*

"Just sit down," she repeats, breaking out in tears.

"Please."

This is the last thing I need right now. I should never have come home so soon.

"Is he coming back?" I ask, stubbornly refusing to move from the doorway.

The phone drops out of Mum's trembling hand. *"No, your father's not coming back,"* she weeps, struggling to form words. She looks down at the floor, resting her head in her palms; her entire body convulsing.

I want to go to her, wrap my arms over her shoulders and tell her that he doesn't deserve us, that the best place for him is the gutter, but I'm too numb, too drained. So instead I just stare at the photo of him on the mantelpiece and pretend that he's a stranger, that he's not the man that I spent my entire life idolising.

He's nobody to me now. Just a man who—

"Your father's dead, Matt," Mum blurts out behind shudders of turmoil.

"What?" I ask with a deep scowl across my brow. *Did she really just say that?*

No, of course not. I'm still high. Still drunk.

He can't be dead.

"They found him this morning," Mum replies. "With a note."

"You're lying," I say, shaking my head. "Why would you say something like that?"

Mum gets up from the couch, eyes streaming, and walks over to me. "It's true, Matt," she says, taking both my hands. "*He's gone.*"

"No," I say, pulling out of Mum's grasp. "He's just with that woman. That's all. He's not dead. *You're a liar!*"

I start to back away towards the front door, refusing to let her lies seep in.

"I'm not, Matt," she replies as she follows me. "They found him by the train tracks."

"No!" I snap, my back against the door, my hand gripping the handle, ready to bolt down the street. "Dad wouldn't do that to us! He wouldn't leave us like that!"

She opens out her arms, inviting me in for a hug. "*Come here, Matt.*"

Shaking my head in disbelief, my vision fogs over, and the walls start to move, pressing towards me.

Mum mouths something else, but I can't hear her words.

I can't hear anything.

The acid in my stomach erupts and I puke up over the floor. I wipe my mouth and then drop to my knees in tears. Mum kneels down beside me, her arm across my back, crying hard into my shoulder.

I can't catch my breath.

I need to get out of here.

I need to see him.

I need to see for myself—because this is all my fault. And if it's true, if he is dead…then I really have lost everything.

ONE

I lift the box labelled 'MATTS SHIT' and take it into the bedroom. Dropping it on the bed, I let out a loud moan of relief. I open the box and rummage through, realising within the first second that this is most definitely *not my shit*.

"Aimee?" I call out.

"Yeah?" she replies from the kitchen, which is so close it feels like she's calling from the same room. "What's wrong?"

"How come this box says 'MATTS SHIT' when it's clearly *your* shit?"

"Are you sure? Have a good look. You know what you're like."

I scan the contents again even though I'm pretty sure that I don't own a *Sex and the City* boxset, a stupid dream-catcher, and a collection of ceramic dolphins. "It's *your* shit. Where are my DVDs?"

I hear Aimee groan as she leaves the kitchen. She pokes her head through the doorway, her long blonde hair clinging to her face, still damp from the downpour earlier. "You probably left it in your car. Just go check." She spots the dolphins. "Be careful with those ornaments now; I've had them since I was five. Put them on the shelf before you break them."

"I'm not going to break them?"

Aimee chuckles. "Yeah, right. You're the clumsiest man in the world."

"No, I'm not," I reply, delicately placing each dolphin on the wooden shelf above the bed.

"Yes you are. You spilled red wine over my parents' new rug—or did that slip your mind?"

"That wasn't me," I reply, scanning the box for the DVDs. "I already told you, the cat must have done it."

Aimee rolls her eyes and smiles. "Yeah, yeah. It's always the cat's fault."

I don't retort, too focused on locating my movie collection. *Where the hell are they?* "They're not here, Aimee."

"You must have left it at your mum's," she replies. "Just pick them up on Sunday."

Exhaling in frustration, I empty the box onto

13

the bed. "I *suppose* so."

"Oh grow up, Matt," she says, playfully, as she returns to the kitchen. "You can watch your stupid films another day."

I place Aimee's DVDs on the shelf and her boxes onto the bedside table. "They're not stupid," I mutter. "*Sex and the City* is stupid."

Aimee's cat comes creeping in, loitering by my feet. "*Out, Luna,*" I whisper. "*Go on.*" He doesn't move, just stares up at me with those cold, yellow eyes. Why anyone would want a house-cat is beyond me. The furry white bastard can live outside as far as I'm concerned.

I should have lied and said I was allergic.

* * *

Aimee crawls into bed next to me, wearing her pink pyjamas and thick blue bed-socks.

"I'm exhausted," she says. "Totally shattered."

"Thought you wanted sex tonight. You know— christen the flat."

"In your dreams," she snorts. "Maybe

tomorrow."

I close my eyes and huddle up close to her. "Maybe I won't *feel* like it tomorrow."

"Yeah, right. That'll be a first."

I smile, open my eyes and then kiss her on the lips. "Goodnight, Aim."

"Good night."

As I lie there, almost drifting off to sleep, I think about Mum. I wonder how she's coping without me. Has she made my room into a shrine yet? Probably. The moment I stepped outside the front door, she threw me a pair of those guilt-trip eyes.

I'm thirty-two for Christ's sake!

Dad would understand if he were still here. And I'm sure he'd be proud of me, even as a hospital porter. It's not exactly a brain surgeon, but it's still a job, it's still money. And I've finally got my very own double bed. No one should have to share a single bed with a girlfriend. No wonder Aimee never liked sleeping over. It's nice cuddling up on a single bed—for about five minutes.

We did think about renting a place first, but getting on the property ladder seemed like the smart move. The flat isn't exactly huge, but it's all we can afford right now. Besides, the other flat downstairs is still unoccupied, so *technically*, we have the whole building to ourselves. I just pray to God the owner doesn't sell it to some weirdo. *Or worse: Mum!* No, she'd never leave Cardiff. She's too much of a—

The sound of glass breaking pulls me out of my thoughts.

Aimee shoots up. "What was that?"

"Don't know. Sounds like it came from the kitchen."

She prods me. "Go check, Matt. Might be a burglar."

"Okay. Stay here," I say, climbing out of bed in just my boxer-shorts. Creeping towards the door, I pick up Aimee's 2kg, pink kettle-bell as a weapon, ready for sudden attack. The bedroom door creaks loudly as I open it slowly. Heart racing, I step out into the hallway, knocking the light switch on. I tiptoe towards the kitchen. The door is already open so I just reach in and hit the light switch.

I pause for a moment when I see the fridge door hanging wide open, and a broken jar of beetroot on the floor; shards of glass scattered, and a pool of dark red juice and clumps.

"Any burglars?" Aimee shouts from the bedroom.

"No. Don't think so. Just a broken jar of beetroot on the floor."

"*Shit*. Not my beetroot."

"Stay in the bedroom. I'm gonna check the rest of the flat just in case." I leave the kitchen and head into the living room. Once I switch the light on I can see that the room is empty, and the window is closed. I then check the bathroom and broom cupboard just to be sure. Both empty. Opening the flat door, I step out onto the pitch-black landing.

"Where are you going?" Aimee asks from the bedroom doorway.

"I'm going to check downstairs."

I reach blindly onto the wall, find the light switch and knock it on. I can't see anyone. Grasping the banister, I peer downstairs. I can see stacks of junk mail by the front door, but can't really tell from here if it's locked or not. Reluctantly, I slowly make my way down the stairs to double-check. As each

17

step brings me closer to the door, I'm annoyed with myself for feeling so edgy. I know there's no one down here, but I still can't shake off these nerves. Must be first-night fears. New home. New neighbourhood. Brand-new worries. Once I'm down, I walk over to the main door and twist the handle a few times to make sure it's locked. Over to the other flat, I try the door. It's also locked. I know it's empty but can't resist the urge to press my ear against the door to listen. Maybe the flat is full of smack-head squatters, or illegal immigrants. Can't hear anything. I give the door a gentle tap. "Hello," I whisper. "Anybody in there?" I listen again but there's nothing. No movement, no voices, no sounds at all.

Relieved, I head back upstairs to our flat. I switch off the landing light and close the door, hooking on the door-chain just in case.

Inside the kitchen, I go over to the cupboard under the sink, dodging the glass with my bare feet, and pull out some kitchen-roll, a dustpan and a small brush. I start to gather up the glass into the pan, and soak up the juice with the kitchen-roll.

"How the hell did that happen?" Aimee asks from the kitchen doorway.

"Don't come in here," I protest, holding my hand out to stop her. "You might cut your foot open. The glass has gone everywhere."

"What about you? You haven't got any shoes on either."

"Yeah, but I'm already in here now. It's too late for me."

"Well that makes no sense at all."

I scoop up the last of the beetroot and glass. "Must have just fallen off the shelf. The fridge door must have been left open."

"*Or a ghost*," she says in a spooky voice.

I snort. "A ghost?"

"It could be."

Dropping the pieces in the bin, I make my way out of the kitchen, and then back towards the bedroom. "You're twenty-four years old, Aim," I say, rolling my eyes. "It's not a bloody ghost."

"Don't be so narrow-minded all the time," she replies, following me into the bedroom. "You don't believe in anything."

"Like what?"

"Well, you laughed when I said that I believed in healing, and you rolled your eyes when you first saw my dream-catcher. Bloody hell, you even think acupuncture is bullshit."

"It *is* bullshit," I say, climbing back into bed. "All of it. And anyway, I seriously doubt that a ghost would want to haunt this shoebox of a flat. There're only four rooms. I can think of better places to spend eternal damnation."

Aimee joins me in bed. "Doesn't work like that."

I chuckle. "As if you know how it all works."

"I don't pretend to know everything." She snuggles up beside me. "But it's good to be open-minded. And don't you think it'd be exciting if we did have a ghost?"

I dismiss the comment by kissing her cheek, and then turn to face the other way. "Good night, Aim."

As I close my eyes, trying to drift off to sleep, I hear Aimee mumble, *"Boring bastard."*

Two

I kiss Aimee as she leaves for work.

I can tell she's jealous that I'm off work for two whole days. It's her own fault. She should have put in for leave sooner. February's always easier to get time off at the hospital. No one takes days so close after Christmas, and normally, neither do I, but with the move, and tidying up the flat, I thought I might as well use up a few.

I take a look around the hallway, at the bathroom, at the living room, and smile. First day alone in the flat. No mother bugging me about clean clothes, always promising to stay out of my room. No neighbour's dog barking outside. No phone ringing every five minutes.

Complete privacy.

I can even stay in my white T-shirt and *Spider-man* pyjama-bottoms all day.

Paradise.

I pull out the laptop from the cardboard box, take it to the bedroom, and then plug it into the wall. I do the same for the printer, and within minutes I'm online. Haven't surfed the Web in a few days, been too preoccupied with the move. It feels like the world has gone on without me and I'm out of the loop. I check my emails, social networks, and various movie sites, which takes me about an hour, and then I'm bored. I spend the next hour downloading a few episodes of *Family Guy* and watching some stupid videos on YouTube. The brightness of the screen starts to tire my eyes so I rub them hard.

Another hour goes by and I'm hungry. Have to stop eating so much. Looking down at my midriff, I inspect the slight bulge. *Oh shit*—don't think that was there before Christmas. Definitely not. Need to get back down the gym. Spring'll be here in no time. I lift my T-Shirt up and see three rolls of flab across my stomach. *Jesus Christ*, those are *definitely* new. I straighten and then suck in my belly. It's not that bad. Just the way I'm sitting.

My phone beeps—a second text from Mum asking if I'm all right. I think about ignoring it again, but then that will lead to a phone call, then a visit, and then a full-blown panic attack.

No thank you.

But she really needs to accept that I've moved on with my life, that I'm not a dumb, emotional teenager anymore, and that Aimee is not some crazy-arse man-eater that all mothers fear—she's the greatest thing to happen to me in years. Yeah, she may be eight years younger, but that suits me just fine. I've been out of the game for a long time, so I've got some serious catching up to do.

I reply to Mum telling her that I'm fine, and then I get up off the chair, releasing a giant yawn at the same time.

I'm hungry.

Inside the kitchen, I open the fridge and scan each shelf. Can't see anything I fancy. *Maybe a ham sandwich?* I kneel down to check the bottom compartment for salad ingredients. I pull out a cucumber and a bag of lettuce. Just as I'm about to stand, I notice a large shard of glass poking out from under the fridge. I pick it up and take it over to the bin. Guess I ain't having any beetroot then.

I prepare the sandwich, lay it on a small plate,

and then carry it back into the bedroom. A small cardboard box under the desk catches my eye. I slide it out, peel off the parcel-tape from the top and then open it. I don't remember packing this; Mum must have done it. Inside, I find a few postcards from Uncle Gary, a couple of videotapes, and a stack of photos bundled together with an elastic band. I remove the band and start to flick through. Most of them are ones of me as a kid, at the park or playing in the garden with my cousin. There're a couple of Dad, as well. I stare a little too long at the one with him and me at the beach; his legs buried in the sand, his forehead burnt to a crisp. Happier times. My throat catches so I move on to the next photo. It's me, mid-teens, full of zits, dressed in black, sitting on Gran's armchair. I seem so different in this, like a stranger. I remember trying to smile that day, but it was too hard back then even to fake it.

The next few are just random ones from parties and weddings, with some just senseless pictures of the sky. The sight of all these photos makes my skin crawl; dragging me back to that shitty time in my life.

Some things are best left forgotten.

I quickly get to the end of the stack, making sure that there aren't any embarrassing ones, or photos of my ex-girlfriend. There're none, so I drop them back into the box, push it under the desk, and then return to the computer.

Another hour or so passes and I can feel the drowsiness start to kick in. I rub my eyes again and run my fingers through my short brown hair. Could easily have a nap right now. I lean back in my chair, yawning, just as a cold rush of air slithers behind me, blowing a few papers off the desk and onto the floor. Turning to see if the window is open, I notice Luna; he's standing in the doorway, staring at me in silence. "Out!" I yell to him. He doesn't move a muscle. *Stupid cat.* The window is closed, so I get up off the chair, gather up the papers, and then check the rest of the flat. When I see that the living room and kitchen windows are both closed, I walk over to the flat door. It's locked. Putting it down to a hidden vent, I make my way into the bedroom. Luna is still standing in the bedroom doorway, staring at my desk—and the papers are back on the floor. Shaking my head in confusion, I nudge the cat out onto the hallway, using the side of my foot. "Where the bloody hell's that draught coming from?" I mutter to myself, looking up at the ceiling and walls for a vent. Shrugging it off as another one of life's great mysteries, I pick up the stray papers and return to the screen.

∗ ∗ ∗

Eight o' clock approaches, and almost to the hour I hear Aimee walk through the door. Thank God for that. Need to get off this couch. I greet her in the hallway. "You're home late, Aim," I say, kissing her on the lips, bursting to give her the good news. "Where've you been?"

She goes back outside to the landing and picks up a large, rectangular mirror, propped up against the wall. "Just picked this up," she replies, sounding out of breath. "Thought it'd look nice in the living room above the fireplace. And look…it's even got dolphins on the frame."

Shaking my head with a smile, I take the mirror from her and carry it into the living room.

"What do you think?" she asks. "Too big?"

Holding it up against the wall, I reply, "No. Looks good. We definitely need *something* in here. Looks really bare at the moment."

Aimee nods and then stands back, tilting her head to the side to inspect it. "Yeah. I like it. Let's put it up."

I set it down against the TV stand. "What...tonight?"

"Yeah. Why not?"

"Well, it's late, and I'm tired."

"*Tired?* Don't be so lazy; you've been off work all day. How can you be tired?"

"I've been tidying the flat."

Aimee looks around the living room, spotting the three large boxes still in the corner. "Tidying? Really?"

"Well I did set up the computer and printer. That took me ages."

Aimee rolls her eyes. "Look, the sooner we get this mirror up the better. Otherwise it'll be sitting on

27

the floor for the next three weeks—like those bloody boxes."

"So you don't want to hear my good news then," I say with a smug grin.

"What good news?" Aimee asks, a confused frown across her brow. But then it suddenly disappears and her face lights up. "You got an interview!"

I nod. "Yep. My boss put a good word in for me. They want me to come in next week."

"That's great, Matt!" she says with excitement, hugging me tightly. "I'm so proud of you."

"I haven't got the job yet," I say, coming out of the hug, "and there're six other candidates competing."

"Forget about them—you'll smash it. I have total faith in you. So how much responsibility will they give you?"

"I'll be working directly under the head of the audiology department, helping her with patient referrals, setting up meetings, admin; that kind of stuff. It's not exactly brain-surgery, but it's much more money—and it's a step up from pushing beds and emptying bins."

"Of course it is. And who knows where this could lead." She kisses me on the lips. "We need to celebrate. How about we watch a film with a few beers?"

"Perfect!"

"But first," Aimee says with a cheeky grin, pointing to the new mirror. "Will you put that up for me."

I sigh loudly. "*Fine*. I'll get the drill out."

* * *

"Where are you going?" Aimee asks as I get up off the couch.

"Getting another beer," I reply. "Want one?"

She pauses the film with the remote and shakes her head. "No thanks. Is there any chocolate left?"

I continue into the kitchen. "No, we had the last the other night," I say, pulling out a bottle of beer from the fridge. "Do you want me to nip out to get some?"

"No, it's okay," she replies with a groan. "I

suppose I'll survive."

Sitting back down on the couch, I notice that Aimee has changed the channel to a cooking show. "What's this shit?"

"*Masterchef*—semi-finals. It's nearly finished. Just want to see which one goes through."

"What about the film?"

"Honestly, there's about two minutes left. Just hang on. The film isn't going anywhere. And it's crap anyway."

I shake my head in disbelief, and then sit back on the couch and take a sip of beer. "Well you picked it."

She shushes me. "Just two minutes."

Rolling my eyes, I take another sip of beer. "Okay, but after this—"

The room suddenly fills with a loud cracking sound.

My heart jolts in fright. Aimee grabs my arm, her nails digging into my flesh. "What the fuck was that?" I blurt out, nearly spilling my drink.

"Jesus Christ!" Aimee cries. "Look at the mirror!"

My eyes widen in shock when I see the huge crack running across the glass, as though someone just took a hammer to it. "How the hell did that happen?"

We get up off the couch to examine it. Aimee prods the glass with a finger. "I don't know. Never seen something like this happen before. It must have been flawed. Or maybe already broken in the shop and we didn't notice... Or maybe an earthquake."

"An earthquake? We live in bloody Wales, Aimee. It's not exactly China."

"Well, whatever the cause...I think I just shit myself."

I start to peel the shards of glass from the mirror and place them on the floor.

"Don't put them on the floor," Aimee tells me, and then runs out into the kitchen. "I'll get you a plastic bag."

She returns immediately with the bag, so I drop the pieces in, until all that's left of the mirror is an empty frame. "Maybe you should take it back to the shop. Get your money back. We could've got hurt."

Aimee carries the bag of glass into the kitchen. "I'm not sure. What if they think I've just dropped it on the way home? How can I prove it? They'll never believe that it just cracked on its own."

Sitting back down on the couch, I take another swig of beer, finishing off the bottle. "Well, it's up to you, Aimee. But I would if I were you. Do you want me to come with you? I don't mind arguing with them."

Sitting down next to me, she shakes her head. "No, it's all right. I'll phone them tomorrow and explain." She glances at the TV. "Shit. *Masterchef* is over. I don't know who went through. Bloody hell!"

I hand her the remote. "Just rewind it back."

"All right," she replies. "But you do it."

"Why can't you do it?"

"No. I'll have to close my eyes in case I see who went through. Don't want to spoil it."

I chortle as I point the remote at the TV. "There's something wrong with you."

* * *

Lying in bed, I listen to Aimee as she sleeps beside me, her breathing soft and hypnotic. I wish I could sleep as well as she does. She can just drop off in seconds. How does she do it so easily? Probably doesn't have as much on her mind. Women never do. All she worries about is what colour to paint the living room, and if *Friends* is recorded.

Although, I couldn't think of anything worse than watching that shit.

Even with the central heating on, I suddenly feel an ice-cool breeze wash over me; my arms plastered in goosebumps.

Please tell me I haven't left a window open. Not tonight. Don't make me get out of bed.

After a minute or so, I sigh, and reluctantly climb out of bed. The bedroom window is definitely closed, so I venture out into the dark hallway to inspect the rest of the flat. I hit the light switch. Nothing happens. *Shit!* Bulb's gone. Already? I'll change it tomorrow. Walking in complete darkness, I reach the doorway to the living room. I feel for the light switch. Nothing happens again. I try the one in the kitchen. Still no light. Bloody fuse is blown—

just what I need.

Completely blind, I head towards the kitchen window. I don't feel any breeze, so I'm pretty sure the window is shut. Reaching it, I touch the glass. It's closed. As I walk, barefoot, across the cold floor, I can't help but worry about any stray pieces of glass still lurking. I still haven't got 'round to vacuuming. Need to do it tomorrow. Don't fancy stepping on one, those glass pieces can get everywhere.

Inside the living room, it seems even darker. Reaching the window, I find it locked as well, so I make my way out.

I freeze at the doorway when I hear something. *Droning.* Like the sound of a radio programme turned down almost to silent. Pulse elevated, my eyes go straight to the stereo and TV. The power is off. *Strange.* Frowning in confusion, I quickly exit the living room.

Pull yourself together! It's the draught.

Just before I step inside the bedroom, I hear a hissing sound in my ear.

Almost words.

My body floods with dread and I sprint across the room and leap into bed, yanking the quilt around me.

I hear Aimee begin to stir beside me, so I cuddle up to her.

The hissing repeats in my head—over and over again. Did I just imagine it? Was it just the pipes? The sound travelling from next door?

Those weren't real words. They couldn't have been.

I stare with wide eyes at the dark hallway, wishing that I'd closed the bedroom door.

Nobody spoke to me. *It's impossible.*

I didn't hear: '*I see you.*'

Just a draught.

THREE

I haven't worn a suit in years. It feels so alien. Adjusting my tie, I notice the time on the wall: 8:10 a.m. I best get a move on.

In the mirror, I check my hair and teeth and then slip my jacket on. Stomach filled with crazed-butterflies, I grab my car keys and leave the flat.

Climbing into my car, I take a moment to settle my nerves. *You can do this, Matt. It's just an interview.* I take a deep breath and think about Aimee. She'll be so happy if I get this job. With the extra money, maybe she can quit hers, do something she really loves instead, or at the very least be able to refuse all those weekend shifts. Four years she's been stuck behind that desk answering phone calls. *Four bloody years.* I don't know how she's managed it without losing the will to live. Those lawyers couldn't do jack shit without her help. Just because she hasn't got a law degree, doesn't make her any less integral to running that place.

I take another deep breath, crack my knuckles,

and then push the key into the ignition and twist it.

Nothing happens. Dead. Not even a wheezing sound.

Scowling in puzzlement, I try again. Still nothing.

"Shit!" I cry, hitting the steering wheel with the side of my fist. "Don't do this to me now!"

I try the ignition a few more times, but it's no use. It's got to be the battery.

"Fuck!"

Patting the sweat that's collecting on my brow, I try to think of a solution.

Taxi.

I pull out my phone and dial the number.

Engaged.

I try another and the call connects straightaway. "*Hello, Mastercabs speaking,*" a woman says. "*How can I help you?*"

"Oh, hi. I need a cab from Dale Street to the hospital ASAP."

"*I'm afraid the next available cab is 9:15 a.m. Would you like me to book that for you?*"

My muscles tighten with frustration. "No.

Thanks anyway."

I hang up the phone and try another.

"*Good morning. Arthur's Taxis,*" a man says.

"Oh, hi," I reply, my voice laced with desperation. "I need a cab from Dale Street to the hospital ASAP."

"*I've got nothing until after nine, sorry. Rush hour.*"

I end the call without even saying thank you, resisting the urge to throw the phone out the window.

Frustrated, I drop my head back against the seat, and close my eyes. *Think!*

Call Aimee?

No, she'd never be able to get here in time. And those arseholes wouldn't let her leave anyway. My stomach starts to tighten with panic. Maybe call one of the boys? There's no bloody time.

Think, Matt! For Christ's sake!

"Useless fucking car!" I scream, opening my eyes and hitting the steering wheel again.

Come on—think!

Exhaling slowly, I try to calm myself down. I could catch the 8:45 train. It'll be tight, but I might just about make it if I sprint.

No—I'm not getting the fucking train.

Sighing, I start to run my fingers through my hair, but then stop suddenly when I realise that I'm messing up the style. I move my head across to check my hair in the rear-view mirror.

"Oh fuck!" I shout when I see someone sitting in the back seat.

Heart pounding, I quickly turn my head to see behind me.

There's no one there.

Jesus, Matt. Sort your bloody head out. You're seeing things.

Skin crawling, I climb out of the car, struggling to shake off the scare. It's at least an hour's walk. *I think.* Maybe I can make it if I run all the way.

"Why does this shit always happen to me?" I say as I dart along the pavement, sweat already pouring down my face, the skin under my shirt clammy.

Forget about your suit and hair. Just keep moving.

Don't stop for anything.

At the end of the street, just before the turning for the park, I glance back at the car, to the empty back seat. The memory of the figure invades my head. I saw a mop of black hair. Was it a woman? Might have been a man. Too quick to make a real description.

Description? Why? It was just my eyes playing tricks, the glare of the sun in the mirror. *Stress.* That's all. It wouldn't be the first time it's happened.

I cross the road and head towards the park gates, praying to God that I haven't already blown this interview.

* * *

I've been staring at the clock for the past hour dreading Aimee's arrival home.

I did think about calling her at the office, let her know I fucked things up—but that would only have ruined her day as well. Bad news is bad news. What's the rush?

The door opens and she walks in, greeting me in the living room, eyes wide with excitement. "Well, how did it go?"

I pick up the remote, pause the movie, and then shake my head.

Her eyes shirk back down as she sits next to me, her hand on my thigh. "Doesn't matter. There'll be other interviews."

"It's not that. I didn't make it—my car wouldn't start."

"Really? What was wrong with it?"

I shrug. "God knows. Battery maybe?"

"That's strange," she says, a hint of suspicion in her voice, "it only had a service last month."

"I know. And I tried to get a taxi, but they were all booked up, so I ended up running all the way. By the time I got there it was 9:20."

"Didn't they still let you do the interview?"

"Yeah, they did," I reply, "but I messed it up. I was so flustered, so sweaty, so *fucking exhausted* that none of my words came out right. I just stuttered my way through the entire thing."

"When will you know if you got it or not?" she asks, stroking my leg gently.

"My boss called me earlier with the bad news."

Aimee sighs, and then kisses me on the cheek. "Don't worry about it, Matt. It wasn't your fault."

"No?"

"These things happen. Cars break down all the time."

I shake my head and lean back on the couch. "It's typical though. It's always something with me."

"What are you talking about?" she asks, taking hold of my hand.

"Well, what about our first date?" I reply. "I almost missed that as well."

"You were late—so what? Everyone loses their car keys. It's no big deal."

"It is a big deal when it's something important."

Aimee rolls her eyes.

"What about our so-called trip to Paris?" I continue. "I fucked that up too, didn't I?"

"Okay, I'll give you that one. Losing your passport was pretty dumb."

"It's like I'm cursed."

Aimee laughs. "Bloody hell, Matt, don't be so overdramatic. So you screwed up an interview, lost a few keys, spilled wine on a rug—big deal. You've still got a job, my parents love you, and more importantly, you've still got me. So stop feeling sorry for yourself and start appreciating how great your life is."

She's right, I know she is, but I still can't shake off this feeling of self-loathing.

The room falls silent.

"Look," Aimee says, breaking the silence, "why don't we just chill out in front of the TV tonight? I know it sucks missing out on a new job, but like I said before, there'll be other interviews, other jobs." She kisses me on the lips. "So don't worry so much."

I manage a smile and then give her a hug. "Thanks."

* * *

"What time is it?" Aimee asks, her words stifled by a loud yawn.

Squinting, I check the clock on the mantelpiece. The only light in the room is coming from the TV and the hallway, so I have to lean forward to read it.

"Ten to twelve."

"Shit, it's late." She gets up off the couch, Luna still asleep at her feet. "Where does the time go?"

"I know." I switch the TV off with the remote and then follow her up, yawning as I straighten. "What's your day like tomorrow?"

"Busy," she replies. "I'm working down the Bridgend office in the afternoon. They're understaffed. *Again.*"

"I hope they're paying the fuel costs. Bridgend's a good twenty-five miles out. It's a bit of a trek."

I follow Aimee out of the living room, into the hallway. "Of course they are," she reassures me. "Seventy pence a mile."

"That's shit. What about the wear and tear of your car? And your tyres."

Aimee turns to me and smiles. "What, would you prefer that I take your *reliable* car instead?"

I chuckle. "I'll swap if you like."

"*Ha!* I'll never get to work with that rust-bucket."

Just as we reach the bedroom, an ear-piercing hissing sound bursts out of the living room—

followed closely behind by Luna. We leap out of the way as he darts past our feet, disappearing into the bedroom.

"Luna," Aimee softly calls out to him. "What's wrong, boy?"

"Stupid cat," I say, shaking my head in annoyance. "The world's first feline to be scared of the bloody dark."

"Check the living room, Matt," Aimee says, following Luna into the bedroom. "Maybe he saw a mouse."

Rolling my eyes, I make my way over to the living room. "A mouse? There're no mice in here. Maybe a spider or—"

Suddenly the entire flat comes alive with a loud, heavy thud.

What the fuck was that?

Frantically switching on the light, my jaw drops wide open in horror. Our fifty-inch plasma TV is lying facedown on the carpet; the cables hanging loosely from its back, wrenched out of the wall and DVD player. I kneel down next to the TV, as if tending to an injured person.

"What the hell happened?" I hear Aimee ask from the doorway.

"I don't know." I take hold of the edge and lift the TV up to inspect the screen. There's a large crack running down its centre. The sight is almost too much to stomach.

I prop it up against the cabinet and stand back.

"How did that manage to fall?" Aimee asks.

I don't answer; just shake my head in astonishment. Can't seem to be able to form any words. Any explanation. Any thoughts. Just...

"Maybe someone from downstairs?" Aimee offers. "Maybe someone hit the ceiling with something."

I turn to her, grimacing. "The downstairs flat is still empty. There's no one living there. It was your bloody cat."

"Don't be so ridiculous, Matt. How could Luna push that a massive TV off the cabinet? He's only small."

"Well why else did he make that hissing noise and then run out of here like that?"

"I don't know," Aimee replies. "Maybe he saw

46

something."

"A mouse didn't push the TV over."

"I didn't say it did."

"Then what, Aimee?" I snap. "A ghost?"

Aimee says nothing, just gives a subtle shrug.

"There's no ghost living in this flat," I announce with conviction, "and there never will be."

"Look, even you have to admit that there's been more than a few occurrences since we moved in."

I snort. "Occurrences? A few broken things, a spooked cat and a cold draught is hardly a job for *Mulder and Scully*."

"What draught?" she asks with intrigue, as if she's stumbled upon a clue to a murder mystery.

"It's just a little breeze coming in, that's all."

"I take it you couldn't find the cause," she says, "otherwise you wouldn't have mentioned it."

"Oh for God's sake, Aimee, can we focus on the problem of the smashed TV, please? This is far more important than some stupid ghost."

"Have you seen anything?" she asks, completely ignoring me. "Heard something maybe?"

I reply with a pissed off groan. The very notion

that a ghost is the cause of all these things is complete and utter nonsense. There was nothing sitting in the backseat of the car. No one whispered '*I see you*' to me, and no bloody ghost pushed over my precious TV.

It was stress, the wind—*and that fucking cat!*

"Must have been a tremor," I lie. She'll only get upset if I blame Luna again.

Aimee chuckles sarcastically. "A tremor? Like an earthquake? Well, that says it all."

"Says what?"

"That you're full of *shit*."

"No I'm not," I snap, checking that the DVD player isn't damaged as well. "I just don't believe in ghosts, so just drop it now!"

Aimee sits on the couch, her breathing shallow, like she's just about to cry.

"I'm sorry," I say, walking over to her. "I didn't mean to sound like a dick. I just don't know how we're going to afford another TV." I sit next to her and put my arm around her back.

Aimee turns to me with worried eyes. "Doesn't it frighten you at all?"

"Frightened about what?"

"The ghost for Christ's sake!" she barks as a teardrop runs down her cheek. "What's wrong with you, Matt?"

A short chuckle unconsciously slips out, so I retract it immediately.

"You might not give a shit," she continues, "but I do. If we do have a spirit, then we've clearly pissed it off."

In my head I'm rolling my eyes. Okay, I'll give her the TV, but I don't know how dangerous a draught and a broken jar of beetroot is. "Look, we're seeing your parents on Sunday. Why don't we ask for their opinion?"

Aimee sniffs loudly, wipes her eyes with her sleeve, and then smiles. "Good idea."

I return a smile. "Come here," I say, pulling her in for a hug, one eye still on my smashed TV.

Ghost.

At least her parents will make her see sense.

FOUR

Aimee's parents' house. Carmarthen. Sunday lunch. Favourite meal of the week for most.

Not here, and not me—or anyone *else* with taste buds.

Swallowing the un-mashed mashed potato, I gave a painful smile to Aimee's dad, Byron. He returns a smile and continues to chew on his lamb chop, clearly struggling to bite through it like a dog with a chew-toy.

Poor bastard. He's got to live with Lynne's God-awful cooking every night of the week. And it's not as if they have the odd night out at a restaurant, or a quick trip somewhere for lunch. This is it for them. Both retired. Both content with staying home all year round. They may go to Scotland or over to Ireland once or twice a year, but they always take the caravan.

Different place. Same chef.

"I'm done, Mum," Aimee says, pushing the half-eaten plate away. "Couldn't eat another bite."

"You've barely touched it, love," Lynne points out as she comes to take her plate, her cream jeans and white blouse clinging to her skeletal body. "Was it all right?"

Aimee nods, eyes wide with false-enthusiasm. "It was lovely, but I'm still on a diet. Plus, my meals have been so small lately that I think my stomach's shrunk."

Lying cow.

"Oh, all right, love." She takes the plate over to the sink. "Some pudding?"

Aimee waves her hands in protest. "Honestly, Mum, I'm full. Really."

Lynne starts to rinse the plate even though no one else has finished. "How's yours, Matthew?" she asks me. "Would you like some more? There's plenty of mash left."

I shake my head as I swallow a piece of rock-hard cauliflower. "I'm good, thanks." I bring my plate over to the sink before she can add any more to it, and slide it into the bowl. "Sit yourself down, Lynne. Let me do those dishes. You still haven't eaten yet."

"No, no. I'll eat mine later. I'd prefer to clean the kitchen before I sit."

"Okay, but let me at least do something."

"No, honestly, Matthew, I'm fine. You just sit yourself down and I'll bring you your pudding. Apple crumble and custard. Your favourite."

Forcing a big grin, I reluctantly sit back down at the table and watch Aimee smirk at me, clearly proud that she evaded another one of her mother's hideous puddings.

I take a sip of wine. It brings me back to that fateful day when I ruined their new rug. That look on Lynne's face still haunts me, as she watched me squirm, trying desperately to mop up the wine with kitchen roll.

Not the best way to meet the parents.

"So how's the flat coming along?" Byron asks me. "Settling in all right?"

"It's fine, thanks," I reply, "apart from one or two teething problems."

"Oh, right. What kind of teething problems?"

"We have a ghost," Aimee interrupts.

Byron's face lights up with intrigue. "Really?

What makes you think that?"

"Well, where do we start?" Aimee replies. "First a jar of beetroot flew out of the fridge and smashed."

"No it didn't," I pointed out with a half-snigger. "It just fell from the shelf. It didn't *magically* fly through the bloody air."

Aimee tuts loudly. "*Fine*. But the fridge did open by itself though."

I sigh, shaking my head. "Look, Byron. A few things have happened, I'll admit that, but there're no such thing as ghosts."

"Yes there are, Matt," he announces to me, leaning forward in his chair. "I've seen one." He looks at Lynne. "We both have."

I swallow another mouthful of wine, realising that her entire family are firm-believers and I don't stand a chance in Hell of talking Aimee out of it.

I should never have brought it up.

Lynne sets down a bowl of hot apple crumble and lumpy, yellow custard in front of me. "There you go, Matthew. Tuck in."

"Thanks," I reply, picking up my spoon. "Looks

great." *It doesn't.*

"Hey, Lynne," Byron says to her.

"Yes?"

"Tell Matt the story about that dead kid stuck in the chimney."

* * *

The drive back is long, dark and silent. Aimee's still in a mood with me for not believing her mum and dad's story. It's a forty-minute drive back to Swansea—so *Thank God for radios.*

Just as we turn off for the city centre, Aimee finally speaks. "You should at least *pretend* that you're interested."

Relieved that she's finally broke the silence (even though it's not to apologise), I turn down the radio to speak. "I did try to pretend. I tried my hardest. In fact, I should have got a bloody Oscar. But there's only so much fake-smiling you can do for one afternoon."

"Well you should have tried harder. I do for *your* mother."

"What are you talking about? Mum doesn't tell us ridiculous ghost stories."

"No, but she bores me with stories about you and your cousins. And bloody cooking."

"Cooking? When?"

"All the time. And the only reason she does it is to have a pop at me."

"Mum would never do that?"

"Yes she does. She knows I'm a terrible cook, and she loves to rub it in."

I shake my head in protest. "You're just being paranoid now. Mum *loves you*."

"I know she does—and I love her, too—but I still have to pretend I'm interested in everything she tells me. Even if I'm bored out of my skull."

I don't respond. It's clear that nothing I say is likely to resolve this argument. And I can see it going off track any second. I know the signs. Plus, she's had a few glasses of red wine—and that's never a good combination. I'll shut my mouth 'til we're home.

We pull up outside our building. When the engine cuts out, so does the radio. And then the silence really hits home. Even the clicking of the door opening is a welcome break in tension. We climb out of the car and then go up to the front door. I'm dying to speak, but there's no point. Not yet anyway. I can tell she's still angry, still after blood.

Climbing the stairs, every creaky footstep is a reminder of what's brewing. Any second now and things could just blow up. I'm too tired to let that happen tonight. And I want sex, so I just have to last at least until we're in the flat and watched a little TV.

TV.

Shit! Completely forgot it was broken.

I squeeze my fist in frustration. She doesn't see it. Don't want her to think it's about her, even though it sort of is. Can't let a lack of TV spoil my evening. Maybe it's better that it's broken; talk things out a little. Who needs TV anyway? I can read a book, or tidy up a little, even have a deep and meaningful discussion about work.

I can use the small TV from the bedroom!

Problem solved!

I push the key into the door and walk inside. Aimee is purposely a few steps behind, clearly still sulking, still holding her ground. Can't even remember what we're fighting about. Something about cooking or... Who cares?

I sit on the couch. Aimee's in the kitchen, opening drawers loudly, cutlery shifting and clunking together, clearly still pissed off. I start to feel drowsy and sluggish. Need to get to bed. Been a long day.

Any hope for sex soon begins to fade, as Aimee still hasn't come into the living room.

Closing my eyes, I think about taking Aimee away somewhere warm. Greece? South of France maybe? Ibiza? Vegas? No, too expensive. Best keep it to Europe. Ibiza sounds good, but am I too old? I'll be thirty-three soon. I'll stick out like a sore thumb. Don't want to be one of those old bastards, wearing a tight T-shirt, lurking in the dark corners of a nightclub.

No, thirty-three's not too old. I just have to know my limitations. Can't be out 'til six in the morning anymore. Been there, done that.

The visions of lying on a sunny beach, drinking cocktails, surrounded by half-naked Spanish girls, are getting more and more vivid. I can feel myself drifting off to sleep. Half lucid. Half dreaming. I can see the water and the expensive yachts, and the blistering sun about to set over the Mediterranean coastline. I can see the faces of couples watching in awe, holding each other tight, watching the sky turn orange. I can almost hear the—

Suddenly Aimee's cold hand on my thigh yanks me back to reality. Away from the beach. Away from the beautiful women. I keep my eyes closed as she works her hand towards my crotch. I can feel myself getting hard. I want to open my eyes, but I'm afraid I might ruin the moment. Just a second ago I was happy to crash out on the couch for the night, but right now all I can think about is tearing Aimee's clothes off and fucking her, right here on the carpet. I knew if I waited long enough, if I bite my tongue, she'd eventually come 'round. She always does. I might be sober but Aimee isn't—and drunk-sex just so happens to be my favourite pastime.

I'm desperate to open my eyes, to throw her to the floor, but I can't. The sensation of her hand, gently stroking my cock is too good. I can feel her fing—

"You coming to bed or what?" I hear Aimee say.

My eyes spring open to find Aimee standing in the doorway, holding a steaming cup of coffee.

Shuffling quickly, I turn to see an empty couch.

"What the fuck," I say under my breath.

"What's wrong?"

Frowning in confusion, I scan the room.

"What are you looking for?" she asks.

I rub my face with both hands, trying to shake off the disorientation. "Nothing. Just thought... Were you just in here a second ago?"

She shakes her head and takes a sip of coffee. "No. I've been in the kitchen. Why?"

"It's just," pointlessly, I give the room another scan, "I could've sworn you were sat next to me, with your hand on my leg."

"No. Not me. You must have fallen asleep."

I rub my eyes and get off the couch, still unable to fully shake off the dream. Still feels so real, so vivid. Can't remember the last time I had a dream like that.

Aimee walks into the bedroom. I follow her in, smiling, thinking about how close I came to having sex with myself.

I suppose it wouldn't be the first time.

FIVE

"So how's that leg of yours this morning?" I ask Mary Davies, as I push her wheelchair towards the X-Ray department. "Still not healing?"

"Sorry, love," she replies, tapping her right ear. "I don't have my hearing-aid in. You'll have to speak up."

"How's that leg of yours?" I repeat, this time much louder.

"It's bloody awful, Matthew," she replies; her elderly voice gravelly. "Just *awful*. And it has been for three months now. I bet you're sick of the sight of me."

"Don't be so silly," I reply, chirpily. "As much as I want you to get better, the place wouldn't be the same without you, Mary."

"Oh, that's sweet. You're a good boy, Matthew. You're all good boys here. I tell you, the porters here are second to none. *Honestly*. Better than those miserable doctors, and those bloody nurses. All I hear is moaning about how tough their job is; but every time I see them they're drinking tea and scoffing biscuits. Not like you porters. Hard at work all the time."

I chuckle quietly. Probably wise not to tell her that I spent most of the morning in the canteen, scoffing bacon and toast with the boys. "Well, that's good of you to say. We do our best."

Around the corner, just past Ward 4, I see Paul coming out, pushing another elderly woman in a wheelchair; this one is at least ninety, and much more frail and withered. "Where you off to, Matt?" he asks me; his bald head in desperate need of a shave; the stubble on his chin bordering on becoming a full-grown beard.

"X-Ray," I reply. "You?"

"*Snap*. Me too."

"Now there's another damn good porter," Mary tells the other patient as both chairs are pushed, side by side, down the corridor. "These boys are the heart and soul of this hospital."

The other patient doesn't reply, just nods, clearly comatose or half asleep.

"So what you get up to over the weekend?" Paul

asks me.

"Nothing much. Bit of shopping on Saturday. Sunday lunch over at Aimee's parents' house. Usual stuff. You?"

"Went out with my brother. Had a skin-full of beer again. Spent most of Sunday suffering on the couch."

"Get lucky?"

Paul smirks. "'Course I did. What do you take me for?"

I shake my head, smiling. "You seeing her again? I mean…is she the *one?*"

Paul chuckles. "What do *you* think?"

"So no then."

"*Damn right.* I can't see me settling down. Can you?"

"Well, definitely not now anyway."

"I mean, Aimee is great, but sticking with the same girl, day in, day out," he sighs, "I think I'd lose it, mate."

We reach the X-Ray department, go through the double doors, and then take the patients into the waiting room. "See you later, Mary," I tell her, leaning slightly in front of her.

"Okay, Matthew," she replies; a big smile spread across her gaunt face. "Thank you my boy."

Paul's patient is fast asleep in her wheelchair, so we exit the department and head back down the corridor.

"So how's Aimee?" Paul asks. "Haven't seen her in ages. You guys settled into the flat yet?"

"She's good. The flat's good. Well, apart from the fact that Aimee thinks it's haunted."

"Really? Since when?"

"As soon as we moved in. I mean, I admit, there have been a few weird things happening, but..." I shake my head.

"Well, maybe you do have a ghost. How old is your flat?"

"The flat is brand new, but the entire building is pretty old. Not sure how old though. But apart from a few noises, a few things breaking, the place is fine. I put it all down to coincidences. That's all. Aimee just loves a good ghost story."

"Look, if I were you I'd do what*ever* that woman says to do. This is the first proper relationship you've had in about fifteen years, so you don't wanna screw things up."

"No, I know. And I won't screw it up. Aimee's awesome. We have our moments, but that's what I love about her. We can bicker about stupid things like money and ghosts, but I still can't wait to see her when I get home."

Paul makes a retching sound. "I think I just threw up a little in my mouth."

"*Dick-head*," I say under my breath.

"And look, as for your ghost problem, I'm with Aimee on this one. Tell her I said that, yeah? Tell her I'm on board."

"Why the hell do you care what Aimee thinks?"

"To stay in her good books...you know, so she'll put a good word in for me."

"A good word in for what?"

"With her sister."

I laugh out loud. "With Nia? As if! You haven't got a fucking chance, mate."

"That's a bit harsh. Why not?"

"Because Nia knows you're a dirty bastard, that's why. Plus, she's got a little girl. Can you really see yourself putting up with a kid?"

"Doesn't bother me in the slightest."

"Bullshit."

"It doesn't. I like kids. I'm good with 'em. You can tell her that from me."

I hear my name being called over the radio. I unclip the radio from my belt and bring it up to my mouth. "Yeah, Matt here, Angela. What have you got for me?"

"*Blood pick up in Ward 3, Matt,*" Angela replies, her shrill voice muffled by the speaker.

"Yeah, no worries, Angela. On my way." I reattached the radio to my belt.

"So," Paul continues, as we both head towards the stairs, "you gonna put a word in or what?"

"What do *you* think?"

"*Prick.*"

Six

It's Aimee's twenty-fifth birthday.

The Cawdor Restaurant is jam-packed. In the lobby there is a large bar with several brown-leather couches, with customers waiting to be seated, and the high ceiling has giant wooden beams across it. Not sure what this place once was or is trying to look like...but it's posh—that much I know.

We follow the waitress to our table. As we both sit, I notice how amazing Aimee looks in her tight-black dress, her normally pale skin seeming a lot darker tonight. Spray-tan? Maybe a quick sunbed session? I wouldn't put it past her, especially on her birthday. I check the time on my phone. Not bad. Only five minutes late. That's got to be a record for us. Aimee picks up the wine list first. "What do you fancy drinking?" she asks me. "Red or white?"

"I was thinking champagne."

Aimee's face lights up. "Really? There's no need to spend that kind of money tonight. It's only my twenty-fifth. Plus, the cheapest bottle is forty-five pound."

I smile, praying my nerves aren't obvious. "Don't be silly; it's fine. You deserve it. You work hard. You don't ask for much. Let me treat you."

"Well, only if you're sure," she says, beaming.

"'Course I am." I pick up the menu and notice how clammy my palms are.

She scans the page. "Jesus, Matt. It's a bit pricey."

"It's fine."

She reaches over the table and places her hand onto mine. "Well, I have to say: you're on fire tonight. I'll have to return the favour later."

I grin as I take a look at the food options. "That's the idea."

When the champagne arrives in the metal bucket, the waitress sets it down on the edge of the table, and fills our glasses. She then takes our order and leaves. I have no idea what most of the dishes are, so God knows what I'll end up with. Usually in my experience, when I can't pronounce any of the food, it's a good sign that it's pretty good. *And expensive.*

"So how was work this morning?" I ask. "Has Becky had the baby yet?"

"No. Not yet. They're taking her in to be induced on Monday. You should see her—she's *huge*. Bigger than Nia was." She takes a sip of her drink and nods. "That's lovely. You can really tell the difference from that cheap shit we buy."

"Yeah. It's nice. Not sure if I can really tell the difference though. It's all the same to me. Just fizzy wine."

She takes another swig. "Not cultured like me. I'm like *Frasier* when it comes to wine."

"*Frasier?*" I chuckle, nearly spitting out a mouthful. "Yeah right. You couldn't tell a Moet from a mango juice. *I'm* the only expert when it comes to alcohol."

"Oh yeah, and how do you work that one out then?"

"Beer of course."

"Beer?"

"Yeah. You put any brand of beer in front of me and I can tell you which one it is. *Easily.*"

Aimee laughs and then scans the restaurant.

"Can't believe how posh this place is. It's so nice. We should come to these places more often."

"Yeah, but there's a good reason why we don't—we've got no money."

"I know. But maybe we should spend our money on less crap and more on places like this."

"What crap?"

"You know what I mean. Like nights out in Swansea with our friends. I mean, after taxis and alcohol, between us, we can easily spend over a hundred pound in one night. Sometimes even more. To me that's such a waste. I think I'd be happier just having friends over for drinks. We always have more of a laugh when we do. Do you know what I mean?"

I lean in over the table, place my hand over hers, and smile. "Welcome to my world: Old age."

"*Hey*, twenty-five is practically a teenager these days. I've got a long way off from catching you up."

"Yeah, Yeah. We'll see how you feel in a couple of years when thirty starts looming. Trust me, you'll be panicking, wondering where your life went. How you ended up with such a George Clooney."

"George Clooney? More like Steve Martin."

I finish off my glass and reach for the bottle again. I can feel a bead of sweat as it trickles down my forehead, and I fight hard to steady my hand as I grab the bottle. Aimee notices straightaway.

"What's wrong?" she asks with a tone of concern.

"Well," I stand up from the chair and walk over to her, my chest tight, adrenalin surging. "I didn't bring you here *just* for your birthday."

"What are you talking about?"

I slowly drop to one knee, completely aware that a few people have noticed, and then reach into my inside jacket pocket. Taking hold of the tiny box, I watch Aimee's eyes widen and glow, and her jaw starts to fall in shock. Holding out the tiny box, I smile, unsure of whether to laugh at the ridiculousness of the scene, or burst into tears at the thought of actually being here, doing this.

I open the box.

Aimee's eyes light up when she sees the ring.

From the corner of my eyes, I notice more and more onlookers. Can't help but wonder if they're smiling at such a wonderful (if not clichéd) moment, or laughing at what an arse I'm making of myself.

Either way, there's absolutely no turning back now. Forget the ring. Once you've gone down on one knee, that's it. Time to suck it up and get on with it.

Strap on a pair of balls.

"Aimee," I say, suddenly feeling a little more confident and less of an idiot. "Since the day I met you, I knew I'd found my perfect girl. You're funny, you're caring, you're not afraid to stand up for yourself—and you're the most beautiful, most precious thing I've ever laid eyes on." I take in a lungful of air, hoping to calm the butterflies. "So, will you do the great honour of marrying me?"

Aimee reaches down to hug me. "*Of course I will!*"

The restaurant comes alive with a sea of clapping and cheering. I've never felt so happy, but equally mortified, in my entire life.

But fuck me—it was worth it!

I take out the ring and slip it onto her finger. She beams as she holds up her hand to inspect it.

"Is it okay?" I ask, still not entirely sure if Mum and I picked the right one.

"Of course it is. I love it, Matt. I can't believe you've done this. I'm really shocked. I never thought..." she stops herself from welling up.

I sit back down in my chair, unable to remove the smile from my face. "You really didn't have any idea?"

"No. None at all. I just thought we'd be having a birthday meal tonight." She glances again at the ring. "I'm shocked. Completely shocked. This is the best birthday present *ever*. I mean it, Matt. I can't believe how thoughtful you are. I love you so much. I really do."

"I love you too." I dowse the adrenalin by downing an entire glass of champagne. "You really didn't have a clue?"

Shaking her head, she swallows a mouthful of her drink. "Not a clue, Matt. Honestly. You know me: gullible as hell. So who else knows?"

"Just my mother. She helped me pick the ring. Wouldn't have a clue otherwise. I'm shit with things like that. If it were left to me, you'd probably be wearing an onion ring."

Aimee chuckles and then looks again at the ring, as it catches the light, glistening. "So when we getting married then?" she asks, her eyes still fixed on the diamond.

And so it begins…

* * *

Aimee holds me tight in the backseat of the taxi, clearly still overwhelmed by the events of the evening. I can feel the aftereffects of the adrenalin start to kick in, making me a little lethargic. I try to shake the feeling off, but the hot air pumping through the car-heater is making it impossible.

I can tell Aimee's a little drunk. It doesn't take her more than a few glasses to get her slurring words. I find it hilarious. She finds it embarrassing.

Sex is definitely on the cards tonight, as long as I can stay awake. Once I'm back in the flat, with the lights on, glass of water, I'll be more than up to the task. After all, how often do you get down on one knee and ask someone to marry you?

Aimee is busy texting someone as the taxi turns down our street; no doubt she's spreading the good news to her friends. I'm sure she'll be on Facebook before the night's through, telling the world how lucky she is, how happy she is. But I'm guessing that it's secretly telling all the women: *'Fuck you all—I'm getting married! And you ain't!'*

Of course the fact that I'm marrying a blonde goddess is pretty awesome, but the first thing that popped into my head when she said yes was: Stag Party! I know it's shallow and immature but no more than caring about a shiny ring on your finger. Women have that. Men have stag parties.

And strippers.

"Who've you been texting?" I ask her. "Your parents?"

"No, just Nia. I was going to wait until after I'd phoned my parents, but she just asked me how my birthday went…and I couldn't hold it in."

"I *bet* you couldn't. What if she tells everyone before your parents find out? Won't they be a little pissed off with you?"

"She won't say. She wouldn't do that. I made

her promise."

"Fair enough. I'm sure she won't have to keep the secret for long anyway."

"*Nope*."

I pay the driver and we get inside the building, heading up the stairs towards the flat. "You texted your parents yet?" I ask her.

"No. I'll call them later."

"Yeah. I bet your mother will cry. Guaranteed." I open the door to the flat. "Do you think your dad will be mad that I didn't ask his permission?"

"No. He won't give a shit. He's not like that."

Aimee closes the door behind her and follows me inside.

I knock the light switch on and then make my way into the living room.

In the doorway, I stop in my tracks.

"Fuck!" I blurt out.

The curtains have been yanked off the rails. The coffee table is on its back, with the two glasses that were sitting on top now smashed on the floor. Our holiday pictures from the mantelpiece have been launched across the room. The DVD player is on the carpet, with the disc-tray damaged.

"What's wrong?" Aimee asks. But she doesn't need me to answer. In a second she knows exactly what's happened.

Some dirty cunt's robbed us!

I race into the kitchen and find all the cupboards hanging open. The one below the sink is even hanging off its hinges. Inside was a range of different cleaning products, bleach, washing-up liquid, all of which have spilled out over the floor, dribbling under the counter and table. The fridge is also wide open, with food flung out across the floor, and jars smashed.

I turn to Aimee, noticing her engagement ring as she puts a hand over her mouth in horror. I take her hands and whisper that everything will be all right. I can feel her body tremble in my grip as she takes slow, controlled breaths.

A sudden jolt of panic hits me and I release her hands.

What if the culprits are still inside the flat?

"I'll check the rest of the place," I bravely tell her, and then motion at the door with my head.

"And I want you to wait outside in case—"

"Luna!" she yells in a frenzy of tears.

Oh shit, the bloody cat!

I put my arm out to stop her racing around the flat. "Go outside, Aimee. It's not safe. I'll look for him."

"Find him, then!" she weeps as she steps out onto the landing. "Please!"

Once I hear her footsteps reach the staircase, I switch the bathroom light on and creep inside, adrenalin still pumping. "Luna!" I call out gently. "Come on, boy. Where are you?" The first thing I notice is the shattered mirror above the sink. I scan the rest of the room, but nothing else seems to be out of place. There's only a minuscule sink, toilet and a bathtub-slash-shower. There's no shower glass or curtain to break. No expensive towel-rail to rip off the wall. Just a tiny room with barely the space to dry your arse, and nowhere for a cat to hide.

I leave the bathroom and make my way into the bedroom. "Luna!" I call out again, switching the light on. Like the rest of the flat, it's in disarray. The bed sheets have been dragged onto the floor. The curtains ripped from the rails. Aimee's dressing table is on its side, with the mirror above it cracked. The wardrobe doors are wide open; the clothes now on the floor in a pile. But for some reason my laptop is untouched. Undamaged. Thank God! I kneel down by the side of the bed to peer under. The thought of seeing some junkie hiding under there, holding a *Norman Bates* knife, sends a chill down my back. Muscles clenched, nervous beads of sweat dripping, I slowly lift the quilt. The first thing I see is an array of shoeboxes. Sliding my hand under, I move the boxes over.

"Oh shit!" I yell when I see two eyes staring back at me.

I scurry backwards in fright, crashing into the chest of drawers.

Luna suddenly comes bolting from under the bed, straight past me and out the door.

Groaning, my hand across my surging heart, I stand up. *That fucking cat.*

"Luna!" I hear Aimee cry with relief from the hallway.

"I told you to wait outside," I firmly say "You

could have got hurt."

She's not listening, too busy kissing the fur-ball's head. But then she stops when she catches a glimpse of the bedroom. I follow her eyes and see her dolphins, each one smashed to pieces, bits scattered over the floor and bed.

"I'm sorry, Aimee," I softly say.

"*That fucking ghost did this,*" she sobs, putting Luna down on the floor.

"Look, you're in shock," I say, steering her away from the bedroom and into the living room. "We both are—so why don't I just phone the police and then maybe they can get to the bottom of this."

She sits on the couch, weeping quietly, while I make the call. As I'm waiting to be put through, it occurs to me that nothing was taken. Well, nothing that obvious anyway. Okay, the TV was old, but they might have got a couple of hundred for it. I notice some coins on the floor, which were on the coffee table. Maybe twelve pound. It's not much, but something at least. The dolphins were worth at least three hundred. And of course the DVD player, worth at least a hundred.

Maybe they left in a hurry, heard a noise and got spooked.

Probably a good idea not to mention Aimee's ghost theory to the police. I'm guessing it might not go down all that well.

Just a hunch.

* * *

The police have been and gone. It took them nearly an hour and a half to get here, but fair play, they did their jobs well, dusted the place for fingerprints, asked if we had any enemies, if we'd lost a door key. You know, the usual shit. Couldn't tell us how they broke in, though. There was no sign of any forced entry, no broken windows. They even accused us of leaving the door open. *Cheeky pigs.* As if I'd be dumb enough to do something like that. Although, I did have to think twice when they asked me. Once someone puts doubt in your mind, it's hard to shake it off. But as I told the cops, I've got no idea how someone might have got in, or why someone would do this to us. I mean, yeah, the neighbourhood isn't that great, but it's not exactly The Bronx.

I bring Aimee a cup of coffee and set it down on the kitchen table. Standing over her, I stroke her hair gently. She's stopped crying now but she's clearly still in a state of shock. "How you feeling?" I ask her. "Any better?"

She nods and then sips the coffee. "I'm all right. It's just…" She fights off another bout of tears.

I pull out a chair and drag it next to her to sit. "Your dolphins," I answer for her.

She nods again. "My grandmother gave me those," she sobs. "They meant the world to me. *And now…*"

I drape my arms around her and hug her, gently shushing her like a baby. "I'm sorry, Aimee. Maybe we can fix them. Glue them back together."

"It's not just the dolphins. It's that fact that someone would pick this of all nights to do it. The most special night of my life: *ruined!* Whoever did this has tainted everything now."

"Try not to think about it."

"And if it was a ghost that did it," Aimee continues, "what does it want with us? To move out?" She sniffs loudly. "You know, Matt, after everything that's happened, selling the place doesn't sound like a bad idea."

"Aimee, let's not start this again. It was kids. Nothing else."

"You don't think it was strange that there was no forced entry, nothing of value was taken, and only my stuff was broken."

I shake my head. "What are you talking about? It wasn't just *your* stuff. The TV and the bathroom mirror were broken. Those things were mine as well."

"Yes, but nothing of sentimental value. Those dolphins were a personal attack."

I almost laugh, but refrain. Now's not the time to make fun of her. Let her have a little fantasy. But we ain't selling the flat, that's for damn sure—ghost or no ghost.

"Look, Matt, I'm scared," she continues, "I don't feel safe in this flat."

"I know," I say with a sympathetic tone, "but you've got to stop torturing yourself with this kind of stuff. It's not healthy."

She doesn't retort. Is she finally seeing sense?

"Try and focus on the positive side," I continue. "They didn't burn the place down, and Luna is fine."

Aimee nods, glancing at the cat as he sits under the kitchen table. I'd love to know what he saw tonight. At least then we could put all this haunted flat to rest. "I suppose you're right," she says, stroking his white fur with her fingers. "Maybe I am over-thinking it all; it probably was teenagers."

Hallelujah!

"Of course it was, Aim. Just a couple of scumbags. And don't worry about the flat; I'll clean it up. Why don't you go and run yourself a nice bath."

Aimee nods again, sniffs loudly and kisses me. "Okay, Matt. Thanks." She gets up off the chair. "I was planning on calling my parents about the engagement."

"Don't worry about your parents. They can wait 'til tomorrow, when you're feeling better. And anyway, it's nearly ten. They're probably in bed knowing them."

She walks over to the kitchen doorway and smiles, her lips puffy, her eyes bloodshot. "Ok. Thanks, Matt. I love you. And I'm still happy about getting married. It's just…"

I return a smile. "I know, Aim. I love you too. Now go," I gesture with my hand for her to leave, "get in that bath and try not to worry."

Aimee disappears out onto the hallway.

Once I can hear the bathwater running, I take a look at the mess all around me. I feel the knot in my stomach return and I sigh.

Fucking bastards!

There's a small pool of bleach on the floor, next to the bottle. It's lucky Luna didn't lick it up. The last thing this night needs is a dead bloody cat. I screw the lid back on, and put the bottle back into the cupboard.

I scan the kitchen. *Where's that mop got to now?*

The sound of Aimee screaming causes me to jolt in fright.

"MATT!" she bellows from the bathroom. "COME QUICK!"

Heart pounding, I bolt out of the kitchen.

Aimee is standing naked in the bathroom, her back against the sink, her eyes enormous with terror.

"What's wrong?" I say, panicked, Luna suddenly by my feet.

"I saw someone," she blurts out; her words shaky as her body trembles.

"Where?"

"In the doorway," she says, pointing at me. "Where you are now."

"There's no one here."

"I'm telling you I saw someone. A woman. She was standing in the doorway. Staring right at me. I swear to God!"

I hand her a towel from the radiator, and she wraps it around her body. "You need to search the flat again. There's someone inside."

"Ok, Aimee. Just stay here and I'll go check."

"No way! I'm not staying here on my own."

"So come with me then."

She nods and takes my arm, staying slightly behind me as I head into the bedroom. Just as before, the room is empty. I open the wardrobe just to be sure, but I know there's no one here.

Back out in the hallway, I open the flat door and scan the landing. Deserted. Once the living room is checked, we make our way into the kitchen. Aimee sits on a chair, nervously tugging on the ends of the towel, her face still pale with fright,

"You all right now, Aim?" I ask, my hand gently stroking the top of her back.

She slowly shakes her head. "No. I'm not. I saw someone standing in the doorway. Plain as you are now. I'm not making it up. *I swear.*"

"I don't think you *are* making it up. I just think you're still shaken up by the break-in and you just imagined it."

"It's not an '*it*', it's a '*her*'," she snaps, "and I didn't imagine *anything*. I know what I saw."

"So what *did* you see?" I ask, pulling a chair out from the table and sitting in front of her, my hands resting on her lap.

"I told you, a woman. Young. Maybe in her late-teens."

"Yeah, okay, but what did she look like?"

"Dark hair. Why does that matter?" she asks, throwing me a pair of angry eyes. "You don't believe me anyway."

"Look, it doesn't matter if I believe you or not. You're my fiancée and I love you. So I need a description of her to tell the police."

"You can't tell the police because they'll laugh at me."

"I let out a long, tired groan. "Let me guess— you saw a ghost?"

"You don't believe me, do you?" she says with a disheartened tone.

"I believe you *think* you saw something."

"But not a ghost?" she asks, pursing her lips. It's hard to tell if she's livid or just disappointed. "So I suppose I'm crazy then, yeah?"

"Look, Aimee, I don't think you're crazy. It's just..."

She looks to the floor, her eyes engulfed in tears. I quickly reach across and hug her. "I'm sorry, Aimee," I tell her softly. "I know you're scared. I shouldn't have questioned you."

"It's not your fault," she sobs, sniffing loudly. "You're right. It must have been the shock of seeing the place in such a mess. I couldn't have seen a girl.

It was just paranoia. I'm sorry for screaming like that, scaring you."

I kiss her head and then stroke her hair. *I know she still believes she saw a ghost—Aimee would never give in so easily.* "Don't be silly. There's nothing to be sorry for," I reply, happy to play along to avoid another row. "Maybe we could stay in a hotel tonight. Or drive to your parents. I'm sure they won't mind."

She pulls away from me, smiles, and shakes her head. "No. I'm fine here. Honestly. Thanks for the offer but I just wanna go to bed."

"Okay, Aim. Sounds like a plan. Everything'll be better in the morning—you'll see. We can tell everyone about the engagement then."

Aimee struggles to smile. It's painful to see but she needs to get over this ghost-shit—it's getting absurd.

We get up from our chairs and leave the kitchen, hand in hand. I switch off all the lights, leaving just the bedroom one on.

Aimee drapes the towel over the dressing-table chair, puts on a set of underwear, and then climbs into bed. I turn off the light and join her.

We lie in silence, holding each other for maybe ten minutes. I'm exhausted but too wired to fall asleep. Can't get the sound of Aimee screaming out of my mind. It's unsettling. And all over a little paranoia. Nothing more. It's fascinating how the brain works, it really is. How we can see things that just aren't there?

As the minutes roll by, I can see more and more of the room. My eyes have adjusted to seeing the furniture and the walls, but it's still too dark to see the mess. Suppose that's a good thing. And if I stare long enough, if I really focus, I can even see a person standing next to the wardrobe.

I squeeze my eyes shut.

It's amazing what a little paranoia will do to you.

SEVEN

Finally it's here! The most important day of anyone's life. The day that every man prays will happen. And when it does, it must be embraced, inhaled...*lived*. It must be remembered for the rest of his life. Every minute should be precious. Every moment should be captured.

And every last drop of tequila must be swallowed.

It's not every day someone gets married to the woman they love. So it's my duty to get as fucked up as humanly possible.

Ed, Paul and me are walking down towards The Lava Bar to meet some of the guys. The sun is still beaming even though it's almost eight. I'm already tipsy after the pre-vodka-shots back at the flat. Ed had puked up and missed the kitchen sink completely. The only thing he didn't miss was Aimee's baking trays. Thank God she's out on her hen party, otherwise she would've throttled me.

We stumble through the pub doors, laughing

about God knows what, and I spot Jones and Mark straight away. It's not that hard; the place is deserted. The bar at the back has just two customers slumped against it, there's maybe fifteen people, including us five, sitting around the tables and on couches. I can't help but feel a little deflated by the lack of atmosphere.

It's Saturday night for fuck's sake!

We sit at the table. There's already a pint of beer and a shot of something green waiting for me. I look around the room with disappointment. "What the fuck's happened to this place? It's dead."

"I know," Jones replies. "But it's cheap."

"Doesn't matter," Ed says. "We'll just get hammered here and then head into town about ten-ish. No one goes out 'til then these days anyway, even on a Saturday."

"Yeah. Plus, we can have a proper catch up in here," Mark offers. "It's always too loud in town anyway. We just end up shouting in each other's ears. It's shit."

I take a swig of beer and smile. "Fuck, we sound like old men."

"Speak for yourself," Ed says. "You're the one getting married. That's proper grown-up shit. Can't see me ever tying the knot. It's too much fun being single."

Mark sniggers. "What're you talking about? You were heartbroken when Stacey dumped you. Crying on my shoulder. Telling me that she was the one."

"Yeah, so?" Ed replies. "I was drunk. That was all bullshit. Can't even remember her surname."

"Bullshit," Mark says, shaking his head, then sipping his beer. "We've all been in love. We've all been dumped, and we've all had nightmare ex-girlfriends." He turns his attention back to me. "Some more than others." I ignore the dig. I've heard it a million times before. "So what I'm trying to say, Matt," he continues, putting a drunken hand on my shoulder, pulling me towards him over the table, "is that you deserve someone nice. Someone like Aimee. We all do. So, what I'm trying to say is," he repeats, pulling me even closer, almost knocking my pint over in the process, "when are you gonna share your beautiful wife-to-be with the rest of us."

Everyone bursts out in laughter. I smile and pull

away from him. "Fuck off ya cheeky bastard," I say, playfully.

"I thought it was the best man's duty to shag the bride," Mark says. "No? Or did I get that bit wrong?"

"Yeah, in your dreams, mate," I reply. "She likes her men butch."

"Butch? You? As if."

"Enough of this shit," Paul interrupts, "time to get these shots down our gullets."

I smile at Mark as I pick mine up. The others follow.

"One. Two...*Three!*"

* * *

The entire night is a haze to me.

I remember leaving the flat, and The Lava Bar, and I can vaguely recall the nightclub. As each step brings me closer (or further) to home, I try desperately not to drop my cheeseburger on the pavement.

Just a few steps away from my street, it dawns

on me: where's everyone gone? How come they let me walk home on my own…and on my stag night? I could've been arse-raped! *Useless fucking friends. Typical.* They get me drunk but get themselves even drunker in the process.

I hope Aimee's all right. Her friends better not have let her walk home on her own. *I'll go ape-shit.* I've told her time and time again to take a taxi— even if it's just a few minutes' walk. Even if it's still light. I mean, it's just not worth it. Not for a woman. And definitely not to save yourself a few quid.

I can just about make out my car, parked about a hundred metres away. Could be two hundred. Everything's blurring into one. *Feel sick.* Must be the burger. Couldn't possibly be the ten shots of tequila and eight pints of beer. I glance down at the food in repugnance, take one last bite, and then launch it into someone's garden. Fuck it. It's not littering if it's food.

At the door to my building, I look up at the flat window, nearly losing my footing as I lean back. The kitchen light is on. Aimee's home already.

Lightweight.

I take out my keys, then drop them instantly onto the doorstep. Bending down to grab them, I suddenly feel lightheaded. *Think I'm gonna puke.* I fight off the sensation. *Can't let it beat me. Not on my stag.* I haven't puked in so long, so I ain't gonna start tonight. I take in a few steady breaths to settle my stomach. It works for a moment but then a rush of vomit bubbles up and bursts past my throat and out of my mouth, spraying all over the floor and door.

When I'm finished, I spit a few times, wipe my mouth with the sleeve of my white shirt, and then pick up the keys, which are now covered in puke. I shake them down, lumps of digested food flick off onto the door, some on me. I don't care. It's too late to care. After several failed attempts, I finally locate the correct key from the bunch, and then stagger inside, slamming the door shut behind me with my foot.

Using the banister like a crutch, I manage to scale the stairs, each step seeming mountainous. Once outside my flat door, I switch the landing light on, and then spend a minute working through the keys again. Why don't they have clicker keys for houses like they do with cars? Just point and click. Simple. I groan because I still can't find the gold-coloured door-key. Did I lose it in The Lava Bar? "Aimee!" I call out, knocking on the door. "Can't find my key!" There's no response. "Aimee!" I repeat, pounding even harder. "It's Matt! Open the door!" Still no response. But then I spot the new, shiny silver key and remember that we had the locks changed. *Eureka!*

I push the key in and then step inside.

The flat feels cold. Too cold for June. "Aimee?" I call out again, just as I notice that the kitchen light is now off. *Is she deaf or what?* I switch the hallway light on and then peek into the living room and kitchen. She's not in either room. Walking over to the bedroom, I glance inside, hoping to see her asleep. The bed is empty, still made. She's still out drinking. Could have sworn I saw the kitchen light on.

I make my way into the bathroom, put the light on and walk up to the sink, holding on to it for extra support. Checking my reflection, I notice my bloodshot eyes. I rub them hard with my palms, and then remember about being sick downstairs. I chuckle to myself when I think of Aimee's expression when she sees it. Suddenly I'm glad that she's not home yet. Wouldn't want her to miss it.

But what about sex? What if she's too repulsed by the sight of it? What if she starts an argument with me? Then what happens to sex? Should I go downstairs? Maybe throw a pan of water over it? Maybe I could do it from the living-room window.

Fuck it. She probably won't even see it. And the pigeons will eat it by morning anyway.

Got to sober up a little. Can't be too drunk. Drunk sex only works if you're at least sober enough to get a hard-on. I throw some cold water over my face, lean in close to the mirror, and I smile to check my teeth. They look okay. Hovering a hand over my mouth, I breathe into my palm, and then wince from the rank stench of puke.

I brush my teeth vigorously and then spit the foamy toothpaste into the sink. "Need a coffee," I mumble to myself as I check my tongue for fuzz. I wipe my mouth and face with the towel, throwing it onto the side of the bathtub, and not back on the rail. I'm sure Aimee won't mind. I leave the bathroom and head towards the kitchen. Once inside, I hit the light switch and walk over to the kettle. I see steam coming out from the top. Confused, I touch the sides of the plastic; it's boiling hot.

"*How the fuck…*"

Scanning the room and out through the doorway, I look for Aimee again. "Aim? You home?" With no response I venture out into the hallway and living room.

The flat is deserted apart from Luna; he's fast asleep by the fireplace.

Just as I'm about to leave the living room to check the landing, I hear a glass smash. My heart jolts! I dart into the kitchen to find pieces of broken glass scattered across the floor. "What the fuck is this shit?"

The wind? But I can see from here that the window's closed. It could be slightly ajar. Each footstep makes a crunching noise as I make my way over to the window. Turning my foot over, I look down at my leather shoe; there are small pieces of glass pressed down into the sole. I push them off with my fingers; don't want to be traipsing it through the rest of the flat. At the window, I see that it's definitely locked tight.

Something hard shunts the window.

"Fucking hell!" I cry out, hand over my thrashing heart. *It sounded like it came from inside.*

Impossible.

I grasp the handle and open the window. Poking my head out, I can just about see the front of the building. I don't see any of the guys, or Aimee. The street seems empty. In the distance, I hear the faint sound of a siren. Not sure what type of siren. Police. Ambulance. Could be either. But that's it. No people. No cars. Not even a dog barking. No signs of life whatsoever.

The entire street's asleep.

Closing the window, I feel the dread start to subside, and my rational thoughts begin to seep through the paranoid, drunken haze. The kettle must be faulty, and the glass must have been at the edge of the counter. My heavy, alcohol-fuelled footsteps must have vibrated through the kitchen. And the loud bang on the window must have been a bird, or maybe a kid threw something at it. It couldn't have come from inside. Impossible.

Aimee's ghost stories are starting to get to me. That's all.

There's nothing here. No ghosts. No monsters. No poltergeists.

Just paranoia.

But what if it's not? What if Aimee is right and the flat *is* haunted?

Don't even think it!

It's bullshit! It's all bullshit!

And we're not selling the flat!

Leaving the kitchen, I avoid the broken glass like land mines, and head for the bedroom. Don't feel like coffee anymore.

I knock off the lights as I go until the bedroom is the only room that's lit. Stripping down to nothing, I suddenly feel that icy chill again. There's a white cloud of cold breath as I exhale, like a puff of smoke from a cigarette. I switch off the light and then climb into bed.

Should I try to stay awake, wait for Aimee to come home? But who knows how long that could be? I glance over at the clock on the bedside table. My vision is still a little blurry, but I think it says 4:31 a.m. *Jesus.* That's late for her. Normally she comes stumbling in at around twelve. Should I be worried? Maybe give her a call? No, she's fine. It is her hen party after all. The taxi's probably delayed, or maybe she's crashing at one of her friend's houses.

Fuck waiting for her. I'm sure she'll wake me when she gets in. She's not exactly renowned for her stealth-like movements when she's been drinking. She'll most likely put every light on in the flat, turn the TV on loud, and cook something in the kitchen.

My eyelids feel heavy. I fight hard to keep them open, to stay awake, but it's too hard. I feel myself drift off to sleep.

Just hope Aimee wants sex as much as I do.

* * *

I'm woken up by the sound of footsteps. Opening

my stinging eyes, I can barely see; my vision blurry, half asleep. The hallway light is on.

Aimee is standing in the doorway.

Don't know if I'm still up for sex. Too tired. Feel like crap. Think my hangover's kicking in. Aimee's drunk, I can tell. The way she's just standing there, staring. Silent. Too hammered even to string a sentence together.

She wants sex. It's obvious. Otherwise she would've just collapsed on the bed, and gone straight to sleep. Closing my eyes, I pray she doesn't bother me. I hate turning down sex, but the room's a little too spinny. I might throw up again.

I hear her footsteps coming towards the bed, softly brushing against the carpet. She's moments from crashing into a piece of furniture. Huddled up on my side, facing my bedside table, I feel the quilt shift. Still with my eyes tightly closed, I feel her weight press down on the mattress. She still hasn't said a word. Probably waiting for me to make the first move. Or maybe she actually believes that I'm fast asleep. I have just been on my stag party. She knows how much alcohol I've probably drunk. But then I flinch as her ice-cold fingers gentle graze my bare-stomach. Her hand starts to move slowly down past my bellybutton, onto the top of my left thigh. The cold sensation is almost unbearable, but I remain still. I resist her lure. Don't know how long for because I can feel myself getting hard.

She caresses my leg for a minute or two, gradually making her way towards my cock. And then she strokes it and I can no longer keep up the charade. Still too dark to see, I turn to face her. I run my fingers through her hair, kissing her lips, pulling her body against mine. I no longer care about my throbbing head, my tiredness, the room spinning. All I want to do is fuck her. Gently scraping my fingernails over her back, down to her leg, I slip my hand under her dress, cupping her arse over her underwear. "I love you," I whisper, as I work my mouth down towards her neck.

"I love you too," she replies softly, barely audible.

She moans gently as my mouth edges closer to her breast. I take my time, teasing her with my tongue, thrusting my hips hard into hers, listening to her—

"You asleep, Matt?" I hear a voice call out from the bedroom doorway.

Suddenly the room fills with blinding light, forcing me to squint my eyes.

A surge of panic and disorientation hits me when I realise that the voice belongs to Aimee. I frantically pull off the quilt, still convinced that Aimee is next to me in bed. But she can't be. *How can she be?*

"What the fuck is going on?" I blurt out when I find the bed empty. "How did you get over there so fast?"

Aimee staggers drunkenly to the bed and sits on the edge of her side. "What're you talking about? I've only just come home." She leans in close to me, eyes glazed over. "Are you drunk?"

I sit up in bed, freaked out, unable to fathom what the fuck just happened. Aimee reaches out and puts her hand on my thigh. I pull away from her. She throws me one of her she-devil glares and then shakes her head. "What the hell's the matter with you?" she snaps, standing up from the bed. "Don't you want sex?" She starts to slip off her dress.

Ignoring her drunken request, I scan the room, eyes focused and wide, stone-cold sober. Not sure what I'm looking for. *Someone.* Anything to explain what I just witnessed. This wasn't a dream. Or a hallucination. And I'm pretty sure that I'm not fucking crazy. Someone was in this bed. With me.

I'm certain of it!

"Did anyone come home with you?" I ask, trying to find some logic in all the madness. "Back here? To the flat? One of the girls maybe?"

Shaking her head, Aimee climbs under the quilt. "No one's with me. The taxi dropped me off just now. Why are you asking such stupid questions? I thought you'd be *begging me* for sex, not boring me to death with all these silly questions." She lies on her back. "Typical man." And then she closes her eyes.

"Aimee," I say, nudging her with my knee. "Wake up. I need to talk to you." Her eyes almost open for a moment, and she mumbles something faintly, but she's clearly fallen asleep. "*Shit.*"

I don't try to wake her, there's no point. I'll get no sense out of her tonight. I'll wait 'til morning, when she's sober. When we're both sober. Maybe in the light of day this'll all make sense. Maybe I'll laugh at how ridiculous it is, and how impossible it is to experience something like that. Something so real. So real I could feel it. Taste it.

Smell it.

I climb out of bed, freezing cold, and dart over to the light switch. I knock it off and then close the bedroom door. Racing back into bed, I shudder as the quilt covers my naked body. Before I close my eyes, before I go to sleep, I take one last look at the room. The moonlight has once again painted the furniture in a shadowy gloom, brought it alive with silhouettes, alive with false-movement. I try to block out the fear as it creeps over me, trying to burrow its way in through the quilt. But I've pulled it too tight. I won't let it in.

I take one quick glance at the wardrobe and close my eyes tightly, wondering if the figure standing next to it really is just my imagination.

Or something else entirely.

EIGHT

I watch as Aimee stirs beside me. I just know she has a hangover waiting behind those blue eyes. I'm tempted to give her a prod to wake her, but I can't bring myself to do it.

Closing my eyes, I try to fall back to sleep. God knows I need it. Didn't really get all that much sleep last night. Not after...

For God's sake! I'm meant to be the logical one. Aimee's the one with the vivid imagination. Not me. *She's* the one who believes in ghosts.

Another twenty minutes pass and I'm still awake. The clock on the bedside table says it's going on eight. Still too early after the shit we drank last night. Not that I can account for every pint of beer and shot of tequila.

Tequila...

The very notion of it turns my stomach. Although, I'm not as bad as I thought I'd be this morning. Thought I was destined for a day with my head in the toilet, but I'm surprisingly fine. Maybe a little rough 'round the edges, but pretty good considering.

Aimee's eyelids slowly part and I get a glimpse of bloodshot eyes. That doesn't look promising. I almost feel sorry for her. Not that I should. It's not as if she hasn't seen me in worse states. Poor girl. Best not laugh. Not yet anyway. It's still early; my hangover may still be waiting 'round the corner. Best not tempt fate.

"What time is it?" Aimee mumbles, closing her eyes again.

"About eight," I reply, stroking her hair gently. "How you feeling? Hungover?"

Aimee doesn't answer, she just grunts and buries her head under her pillow.

"I'll take that as a 'yes' then?" I say, unsympathetically. "You want some water?" Picking up the half-full glass from my bedside table, I hover it above her. "I got some earlier. It's still pretty cold."

She grunts again and attempts to shake her head from beneath the pillow. I chuckle to myself as I return the glass to the table.

Sitting up in bed, silent, I think about last night. I try not to but it's swirling around in my head, nipping away at my rationality.

Perhaps another ten, fifteen minutes pass and I still haven't asked Aimee what I've been desperate to ask her all morning. I'm starving but I know if I get up, eat something, take a shower, I'll never get 'round to it.

"Aimee?" I whisper. "You awake?"

Groaning, she turns onto her side, away from me. I'll be the first to admit that I'm no expert on the female species, but I'm pretty sure that means: *fuck off*.

But I am an expert in persistence. "Aimee," I lie on my side facing her, "tell me what you know about ghosts."

Pulling the pillow away from her face, she slowly opens her eyes. "Ghosts?"

I nod. "Yeah. Ghosts."

Aimee closes her eyes and then pulls the pillow back over her face, and turns away. "Piss off," she says, her words gagged. "I'm not in the mood."

"I'm not teasing you. Honestly. I'm being

serious."

"Look, Matt, I've got a stinking headache and I feel sick—*so leave me alone.*"

"Aimee, I'm not playing around. Please…I saw something…last night. In the flat."

She pauses for a moment, and then removes the pillow from her face and turns to me. "What did you see?"

I shrug my shoulders, still unsure of whether or not I did experience anything at all. "I don't know. But there was something strange in here last night."

Clearly intrigued, she sits up in bed. "So what happened?"

"Well, I'll be the first to admit that I was pretty drunk last night. We must've gone through a fair few tequila shots and beer even before we left the flat. I lost the guys somewhere and headed off home. When I got here, the kettle started to boil…*on its own.* Then a glass smashed in the kitchen. Then I went to bed. No wait! Something hit the window. It sounded like a fist."

"A fist? Maybe someone threw a stone at it from outside. Or a bird could have flown into it."

"It sounded like it came from inside the flat."

"How drunk were you?" Aimee asks, mistrust in her tone. It annoys me because I'm meant to be the bloody sceptic.

"Like I said, I admit I was drunk—but not paralytic. I went to bed, waited up for you—and that's when it happened." I stop for a moment, realising how stupid all this sounds spoken aloud, like a dream you're positive could be the plot of an awesome movie, but then it actually seems God-awful when you tell someone. I mean, am I really going to tell—my future bride—that a ghost tried to have sex with me?

"So what happened?"

"I saw someone—standing in the bedroom doorway. First I thought it was you, but then the figure disappeared."

Aimee's reddened eyes are wide with curiosity.

"And you hadn't fallen asleep?" she asks. "You know, before I got home? You hadn't just *dozed off a little*? Dreamt the figure?"

"Well, I suppose I did doze off a little just before. But then I woke when I thought you were home."

"So how do you know you still weren't half-asleep? It could've easily been a dream."

"Because it wasn't. I was wide-awake. And I definitely saw something."

Definitely?

What the fuck am I saying?

Of course I didn't 'definitely' see something. How could I? That would mean that I *definitely* believe in ghosts—and I don't. It's ridiculous. There must be some rational explanation, something obvious that I've overlooked.

"Look, you know how I feel about ghosts," Aimee says, "so there's not much more I can say on the subject. If you saw something that can't be explained, then it must be a ghost."

"What if someone spiked my drink when I was out?"

"With what?"

"I don't know," I shrug. "Maybe LSD."

"Who the hell's gonna spike your drink?" she asks with pessimism in her voice. "Your friends?"

"Maybe. You know what they're like."

"Yeah, I know what they're like and I know that no one would do something that dangerous— especially on your stag night. *And* so close to the wedding."

"Someone else could have slipped it into my drink."

She chuckles. "With you? As if. I've never seen a drink leave your sight in all the time we've been together. You take it to the toilet; you take it to the dance floor. There's no way someone would've been able to slip it in without you knowing."

"Well, I was pretty hammered last night."

"Look, Matt, why are you trying to talk yourself out of seeing something? A minute ago you seemed convinced that you saw a ghost. Why else did you bring it up in the first place? We both know that things have been happening in the flat ever since we moved in. And okay, I'll admit that some of the things can be explained—but not everything. There's just been too much unexplained stuff. Glasses smashing. The so-called 'break in'. The mirror cracking. And now both of us have seen something in the flat. I mean, come on, I know I

114

can get a little obsessive when it comes to ghosts, but even you have to accept that there's something odd about this place."

She's right—I know she is—but it's too hard to give in. For a moment there I almost convinced myself that the figure by the bedroom doorway was all I actually saw. But it wasn't. There was something in bed with me. Someone's cold hands were all over me. It wasn't a dream. It wasn't the alcohol. And it definitely wasn't LSD. This was something else. Something inexplicable.

"Ok, Aimee," I say, defeated. "You win. I'll admit it: I think we have a ghost."

"Finally!" Aimee screams at the top of her voice, but then places her hand over her forehead and closes her eyes, sinking back down into the pillow. "Shouldn't have done that," she says quietly. "Think I'm gonna be sick."

* * *

I spend the next ten minutes sweeping and vacuuming the broken glass from the kitchen floor.

I know I should put some shoes on, but I can't seem to find the energy. I'll just have to avoid impaling my foot on a piece of shattered glass; keep on the lookout for any stray bits. It's not exactly the first time I've risked it through sheer laziness, and it definitely won't be the last.

Before I put the vacuum away, I drop to one knee, tilt my head to one side, low to floor, and have one final scan for any wandering shards. When I see that there're none, I put everything back into the hallway cupboard, and sit on the living-room couch.

Still no sign of any hangover. Can't say the same for Aimee though. She's spent the last two hours running back and forth to the bathroom. I feel sorry for her, but rather her than me. Can't quite believe I threw up last night, haven't done that for so long. But it's always easier drunk—less to think about.

"How you feeling?" I ask Aimee as she hobbles into the living room; still wearing her pink and flowered pyjamas and thick bed socks; her fringe damp and stuck to her forehead. "Any better?"

All she can muster is a subtle nod as she sits next to me, collapsing into the cushions.

"That bad is it?" I ask, stroking her leg softly.

"I'm all right. Feel much better now. Think it was those cocktails Jackie bought. And those bloody shots of whiskey."

"Whiskey?" I say, shaking my head in repulse.

"I know. Disgusting. They know how much I hate the stuff." She gags briefly, holding a hand over her mouth. "Let's not talk about whiskey."

"Okay. Fair enough," I reply, grinning.

"Let's talk about how it feels," she says, smugly.

"How 'what' feels?"

"To finally believe in something out of the ordinary."

"Fine," I reply with a shrug. *But it feels a million miles away from fine.*

"Look, Matt, it's been really hard trying to convince you that we have a ghost. It made me feel so alone."

"I know, and I'm sorry that I ever doubted you. But it's hard for me. Something like this has never happened to me before. I mean, you know what Mum's basement is like—it's creepy as fuck. And even though I used to hate going down in the dark,

117

I never saw or heard a single thing. Probably the only real fear down there was the huge, grotesque spiders."

"That's fair enough. I get why most people don't believe...but now you do."

"Well...sort of."

"What do you mean, 'sort of'? You just told me you believe in them."

"I know I did, but that doesn't mean that I'm still not open to some other, rational explanation for what's been happening here. Don't you think?"

"Not really. I know what I saw in the bathroom—and you know what you saw in the bedroom. Our flat is haunted. Face facts. And we have to live with that."

"Why? Can't we just throw some holy water over everything, you know, like in *The Exorcist*?"

"Well, firstly, that was a girl possessed by a demon. That's not what's happening here."

"So what is it then? A poltergeist?"

"Maybe. I'm not sure."

"Maybe that's why the last TV fell. Some evil spirit was trying to suck us in. And plus, you work with that dwarf woman. Stick a pair of glasses on her and we've got ourselves the *real deal.*"

"Rachel's not a dwarf. She's just a little short."

"A little?" I chortle.

"Look, forget about movies," she says, impatiently. "Half the stuff is bullshit anyway."

"Yeah, but the other half isn't. Maybe we could get some holy water from *EBay*, and get on *YouTube* for tips on exorcisms. Shit, I bet you could get some priest to *Skype* the ritual on the laptop, save him coming all the way from The Vatican. Christ, I bet there's an app for it, too."

Shaking her head, she scowls at me. "Look, I'm not talking to you about it if you're gonna be like this. This isn't a joke. We're not talking about the odd noise here; we're talking about something nasty living in our home. What if the TV had landed on Luna? Or the boiling kettle spilled over you? Whatever's in here clearly wants us to leave—so cut the bullshit, Matt."

"All right. I'm sorry," I reply, showing her my palms in surrender. "So tell me what you think this is then. Who's haunting us? Someone we know, like a relative? Or is it some dead previous owner with a grudge?"

"I'm not sure. Most likely someone who lived here before us. Some pissed off ghost who wants their flat back."

"So what do we do now?" I ask. "Get a real expert over to check the place out?"

Aimee nods. "Yeah. My mother knows a medium. I'll ask her to get his number."

"Good idea."

Even through all the madness, I can feel my stomach rumble. I squeeze her thigh gently and then get up off the couch. "You hungry? You think you can keep something down?"

Aimee ponders for a moment before answering. "Yeah, maybe some toast. Nothing too greasy. Don't really feel like anything, but I still think I need to eat something."

I nod and then kiss her on the lips. "Ok, Aimee, I'll get you some."

"Thanks," Aimee replies, smiling. "I need looking after today."

I exit the living room and head for the kitchen.

Inside, I pop the bread into the toaster and then put the kettle on. "You wanna coffee or something?" I call out to Aimee.

"No thanks," she replies. "Just a glass of orange juice. With ice."

Once the toast is ready, I bring them both to her in the living room. Aimee smiles as she takes the plate and glass from me.

* * *

It's almost four o clock and we haven't moved from the couch. Aimee's legs have been resting on my lap for so long, I've lost all feeling in my thighs. And my thumbs are aching from massaging her feet for a good hour. She's felt like shit for most of the day, and I've felt pretty good, so it's the least I can do.

Every few minutes, when we're not talking, when there's not something interesting on screen, I can feel last night's events worming their way into my thoughts. That thing in my bed felt so real. I know there's a strong possibility that I was half-asleep, still drunk from the stag—but no nightmare, no trick of the eyes has ever felt so real.

"I'm getting a coffee," Aimee says as she swings her legs onto the floor. "You want anything from the kitchen?"

"I'll get it for you," I offer, hoping she doesn't see past my empty gesture. I half get up from the couch.

"Don't be silly. I'll get my own."

"Are you sure? I don't mind."

Holding a hand out in protest, she stands up and then makes her way towards the doorway. "I'm fine. Do you want anything?"

"No thanks," I say, happily sitting back down, watching her as she leaves the room. "Maybe some biscuits," I call out to her. "Chocolate."

"Okay."

Suddenly there's a loud cry coming from the kitchen.

Leaping up, I sprint out of the living room, into the kitchen. Aimee is sitting on the chair, her left foot up onto her right thigh, with a large shard of broken glass sticking out of her sock. My stomach turns with the sight of so much blood; a small pool has gathered on the floor, and her thick sock is soaked through.

"Shit," I say, as I race over to her. "I'm so sorry. I could have sworn I got all the glass. I even vacuumed the entire floor to make sure."

"Don't worry about it," she says, her eyes watering, clearly in pain. "It was an accident."

"I'm really sorry. I feel terrible. Should we go to the hospital? Looks pretty deep."

Shaking her head, she pinches the fragment with her thumb and index finger, and then slowly pulls it out. Wincing, she puts it on the table, blood dripping from its razor-sharp edge. I carefully remove her sock and then grab a tea towel from the radiator, wrapping it around her foot. She winces again when I apply a little pressure on the cut.

"You okay?" I ask her, already knowing the answer. "Don't want you limping next week in the church."

She sighs lengthily and then puts on a brave smile. "I'm fine. It's just a little cut."

"Don't know how this could've happened," I say, taking the glass over to the bin beneath the window, and then dropping it in. "I swept up and vacuumed. I swear to God. I was thorough. I mean, *really* thorough."

Aimee gets up from the chair and starts to hop towards the hallway. "Don't worry about it, Matt. It's not your fault. I've done it loads of times. Honestly, I'm fine. It's no big deal."

Following her out towards the bathroom, I take her arm to steady her. She smiles at me with a look that says I'm being overprotective. But how can I not be? It was my fault. I missed the glass. Simple as that. Probably still too hazy to see the bloody thing.

Standing at the bathroom doorway, holding on to its frame, I watch guiltily as she takes the tea towel away from her bloodied foot to clean it. The sight makes me gag. I cover the action with my sleeve, and then go back to the living room.

I sit back on the couch, trying desperately to be taken away by the nature show on TV. It's about spiders.

I hate fucking spiders.

* * *

It's going on ten. Aimee's been sleeping in bed since eight. What a shitty day she's had. Bad enough puking and feeling like crap, but then she goes and steps on bloody glass. For fuck's sake. How could I miss such a big piece?

Stupid.

Return of the Living Dead is almost finished. I've seen it God knows how many times. But that's me; can't resist a good eighties horror movie.

Even though I can't imagine being able to sleep tonight, my eyes are burning. Really need to go to bed but can't be bothered. Really fancy something to eat but the kitchen seems too far. I think I'll just stay here and fall asleep in front of the TV, like I used to do back home in Mum's, watching rubbish until three in the morning, and then getting up for school at seven.

Once the credits roll, I start to channel surf. There's never anything on. All these shows, and still nothing good to watch. Too much choice. It was easier when we just had four channels. I'd sit through almost any old shit. It didn't matter if it was a chick flick or a quiz show. As long as it was on the screen, I'd watch it.

I mute the TV when I hear the loud knocking on the door.

Someone's out on the landing. Frowning, I get up from the couch, holding back the butterflies in my gut. I pretend that I'm just a little annoyed that someone has had the cheek to call 'round so late.

How the fuck did they get up the stairs without me buzzing them in?

Twisting the lock, I pull the door open. There's no one out there. Just darkness. I reach into the landing and press the switch on the wall. The light comes on but the landing is deserted. Walking to the banister, I peer over, looking down at the lit up hallway and main entrance. It's also deserted.

"Hello," I call out, half-whispering. "Anybody there?" I listen out for any response. There's none, just eerie silence.

Maybe someone's finally moved in to the other flat. I creep downstairs, no longer able to keep the butterflies at bay. Halfway down, I can see that the flat door is shut. "Hello? Anybody down there?"

Pointing my ear towards the empty flat, I listen out for a voice. But there's still nothing. Not even a little movement. I don't want to go all the way down and knock. I'm too tired and there's no point.

Of course there's a point. Someone just knocked on the bloody door. You didn't imagine it. You didn't dream it. Someone's down here.

Sighing loudly, I quickly walk down the remaining few steps and go over to the other flat. I give a gentle tap on the door, put my ear against it to listen. I hear nothing, so tap a little harder.

After a few more attempts, I race back up the stairs, turn the light switch off as I reach my door, and then close it behind me.

It's not a ghost.

Ghosts don't need to knock. They can move through walls. Why the hell would they knock?

Trying to shake off this cold, creeping feeling I have over my skin, I make my way back into the living room and sit on the couch. I pick up the remote control and channel surf again.

KNOCK! KNOCK! KNOCK!

My body clenches in fright, but I race to the

door nevertheless. Unlocking it, I swing it open wildly, hoping to catch the culprit in the act. Switching on the landing light, once again I see that it's deserted. I go back over to the banister. "Who's down there?" I shout, this time unconcerned with waking Aimee. "I'm calling the police." Maybe a minute passes, waiting for a response, but there's nothing. Just silence. My heart is pounding, and my sweaty hands are trembling. I try to disguise them by making tight fists. I walk back over to the doorway, switching off the light as I grasp the door, getting ready to close it. Scanning the landing one last time, I can feel my heart rate start to slow a little.

KNOCK! KNOCK! KNOCK!

"Jesus fucking Christ!" I scream when I feel the door vibrate in my hand. I slam it shut, heart thrashing even harder against my chest. And then I race back into the living room, body convulsing in terror.

"What the fuck was that?" I mutter, trying to control my erratic breathing. Wide eyes glued on the door, body frozen, I wait for another knock.

Nothing.

I keep waiting.

Perhaps five minutes pass, and I'm just about ready to move. Fuck staying in the living room alone. Not tonight anyway. I'll feel safer in bed with Aimee—even if I can't sleep a wink.

Racing out of the living room, lights and TV still on, my body tightens as I slip past the flat door. Once inside the bedroom, I close the door behind me and slink in the darkness to the bed, stepping on various items of clothing on the floor. I climb under the quilt and huddle up close to Aimee, her warmth soothing the tension in my body. I close my eyes, hoping that sleep will just come instantly. I'm working at six anyway, so at least I'll be up and out of here in a few hours. I'll just have to ignore what happened and think of something else. The wedding maybe. My speech. No, not the speech. Too stressful. The honeymoon? Yeah, Cancun. That's better. No, fuck the holiday. I need to think about absolutely nothing. Clear my mind, otherwise I'll never get to sleep. Think of nothing. Think of blackness. Think of emptiness. Forget about everything.

Forget about the ghost.

It's not real.

It can't be.

Too frightened to open my eyes, even in the darkness, I listen to the stillness of the room. I can just about make out the sound of the TV in the distance. Is that laughter I can hear? A sitcom maybe? Could be. Sounds like it. Suddenly I feel a little less terrified.

Need to sleep.

Things will be different in the morning. Things are always better in the light of day. Much better.

In my head, I hear the knocking on the door. It keeps repeating over and over again.

I ignore the horrid, gut-wrenching sound and try to sleep, holding on to Aimee's body as if my life depended on it.

NINE

I somehow managed to get out of work on time today. Twenty past two is pretty good going these days. Aimee doesn't even know I'm driving up to Cardiff. She thinks I'm in the flat all day. I think she'll understand why I have to see Mum. Haven't seen her in weeks, and she's only been to the flat once. She's always asking about it, always offering to come down, but we're always too busy with something.

The traffic is moving pretty slowly when I hit Cardiff city centre, but I don't mind. What's the rush?

Dad pops up in my head just as I drive past his old office. I hate the sight of the grey-old place, bringing back those awful memories. I swallow the lump in my throat and focus on the road ahead.

I turn the car down Lewis Road, onto Bridge Street, and then home. Well, sort of. Not anymore.

"Oh my word," Mum says as I get out of the car. "There's a sight for sore eyes." She kisses me on the cheek even before I'm out of the car. She's clearly been waiting by the window, watching the street for me to appear, timing the journey to the nearest second.

That's Mum. And she'll never change.

"Hi Mum," I say, hugging her. "How've you been?"

I close the car door and follow her up the drive. She points to the perfectly groomed front lawn. "Just had the grass re-turfed," she informs me, proudly. "And Lloyd from across the road—you remember Lloyd don't you, Matt?"

"Yeah. 'Course I do. I haven't been gone *that long*, Mum."

"No, I know. Well, it feels like forever. Anyway, Lloyd's been helping me with my new flowerbed." She points to the top of the lawn.

"That's nice of him," I say. I've lived with this woman for practically my entire life—she knows that I don't give a shit about gardening.

I follow Mum into the house and we sit on the couch. She picks up the remote control from the side of the leather couch and mutes the TV. It always feels strange when I'm here. *Home.* Even though I'd always be welcome back, I still can't help but feel like a guest. Probably 'cause Mum keeps changing everything 'round. There's guaranteed to be some piece of furniture moved, or replaced with another. The cream-coloured carpet has gone through at least two different shades in the last two years. And that black bookshelf next to the TV was definitely oak before I left. Don't know why she bothers; the house has always been fine. Never dated. Always modern and spotless from top to bottom. Out of everyone in the family, we were the first to get a flat screen TV, and most certainly the first to get an icemaker fridge/freezer.

"Where's Max," I ask, scanning the room for the dog.

Mum's smile suddenly vanishes. "He died."

My stomach flips a little when I hear her soft, morbid words. "Died? How come?" I ask, trying not to seem too upset; I can tell by Mum's eyes that she's been through it already.

"Lung cancer."

"Really?"

133

Mum nods, her eyes clearly burning with grief. I feel guilty for bringing down her chirpy mood—but how was I supposed to know?

"Jesus," I say, placing a hand over hers. "When did this happen?"

"Three weeks ago."

"Oh, Mum, I'm so sorry. Why didn't you say something?"

Mum forces a smile. "What—and spoil your wedding? Don't be so silly. He was eleven. That's not bad for a dog. Plus, he had a good life. And at least he had you to play with."

"Yeah, I suppose, but, I mean…how've you been coping on your own?"

"I've been fine, Matt. Don't worry about me. I do have a life outside this house you know."

"I know you do, but…"

"But nothing. I've got friends. Neighbours. My sisters. And it's not like you're living on the other side of the world. Swansea's only forty minutes away."

"Yeah, I suppose so," I say, ruefully, knowing damn-well that I haven't been paying much attention to her at all, otherwise she would have told me about Max weeks ago.

"So how are things going with you and Aimee?" Mum asks. "Any problems?"

"Everything's fine." *Here it comes.*

"So you're getting along okay, then?" she asks with a tone of pessimism.

Right on bloody cue. "Of course we are. We're getting married."

"I know that, but there's a lot of pressure when it comes to weddings. I know what it's like—and I know what *you're* like."

I roll my eyes. "Mum—Aimee and I are fine. You don't have to worry about us."

"I'm not worried about Aimee—I'm worried about you."

"Well don't be. Things couldn't be better."

Mum taps me on the thigh and beams. "Okay, boy. Just remember that you've always got a home here—if things ever get too difficult."

I return a smile but it's fake. She needs to relax, think about herself for a change. I'm not a kid anymore—I can take care of myself.

"How about a cup of coffee?" Mum asks, getting up off the couch, quickly changing the subject.

"I'll get it, Mum," I say, half getting up. "Sit back down."

"Don't be silly," she puts her hand out in protest, "I'll get you a coffee."

I smile and nod. "Yeah, okay. Two sugars then."

"I know how many sugars you take, Matt. Mother's never forget."

"Tell that to Aimee," I shout out as Mum disappears through the glass doors, into the kitchen.

"So how's the hospital treating you?" Mum yells. "Any promotions on the horizon? Maybe one of those supervisor posts?"

"No, Mum," I say; the memory of my doomed interview stabbing at my thoughts. "Nothing yet."

Mum pokes her head out from the kitchen. "Well, keep your eyes open then. You never know what's 'round the corner." She disappears again. "I'm still proud of you, whatever you decide to do. Always proud how far you've come. Dad would be as well. *Really* proud."

"Thanks, Mum," I reply, spotting a picture of him on the mantelpiece, the one from his Scottish hike. "Means a lot."

Mum re-enters the living room carrying a tray containing two mugs of coffee, and a small plate filled with chocolate biscuits. I take the piping hot drink and set it down on the coffee table beside me. She does the same, using the telephone stand beside her.

"Biscuit?" she offers, pointing the plate at me as she sits down next to me. "Chocolate."

Hesitating for just a moment, I take two from the plate and smile. "I shouldn't really. I'm trying to cut down."

"Why?" Mum asks, her voice high-pitched. "There's nothing of you."

"We've got Mexico in a week. Don't fancy looking all flabby out there. There's only so much gut I can suck in."

Mum chuckles as she takes a bite of a biscuit. "Don't be silly. No one's going to care. Everyone's too busy avoiding drug-dealers and sharks.

Chuckling, I shake my head and then pick up my

mug of coffee. "Mum, you're bloody nuts. You know that, don't you?"

"I'm just saying: be careful out there, Matt. That's all."

"I know you are, but I'm not stupid. Don't worry."

"All right, boy. So what's brought you up here then? I'll be seeing you in a few days for the rehearsal." ·

"No reason. I had some time to kill after my shift. Just thought I'd call up to say hello. Can't a son just pop over to see his mother?"

"Of course you can, boy. And don't get me wrong, I'm glad of the visit—but I thought you had a lot on your plate."

"I just fancied a chat."

Mum grins, puts her hand on mine and gently squeezes it. "Oh, that's nice, Matt. Yeah, you're right: we won't have much of a chance to catch up in the rehearsal. Aimee's parents will be there; and your best man." She sips her coffee and then takes another biscuit. "Speaking of best men: how's Ed's speech coming?"

"His speech?" I reply with moan. "I'm dreading it beyond belief."

* * *

Once I'm back on the road, I listen to the radio. Nothing the station plays is quite my cup of tea but I sing along anyway. For the first time ever, I decide to take the back roads home; avoid the motorway for a change. What's the rush? Motorways are always so mind-numbingly boring. Plus, there's a good chance I'll stop in a service station and stock up on junk food. *Fuck that.* I've eaten way too much shit today already. I prod my stomach. Shaking my head in disappointment, I imagine all those cut-to-shreds bodybuilders, prancing along the beach in Mexico. And there's me, passing out from sucking in my gut to save face. Even though the guys and me always make fun of those roided-up idiots, we all secretly would kill to have a six-pack and guns like Arnie.

On the way, I stop off at Ed's restaurant for a chat. I stay for maybe thirty minutes, but then head off when I see how busy he is. Nearing Port Talbot, I pull into Burger-Land. *More fucking junk food.* I contemplate just using the Drive-Thru, but change my mind last minute and have a sit-down meal instead. They've got computer tablets there now—they've gone up in the world since I worked here. Finishing my food in just a couple of minutes, I spend the rest of the forty-five minutes surfing the net, just looking at any old shit.

I check the time on my phone. It's going on seven. Can't believe how late it is. I notice four missed calls from Aimee. Redialling her number, I wait a few seconds for the call to connect.

"*Hi Matt,*" Aimee says. "*Where are you? Thought you finished work at two?*"

"Yeah, I did. Just been to Mum's. Having a bit of a catch up before the wedding. Why? What's up?"

"*Nothing. Your Mum just called the house asking if you got home safely.*"

"Really? Jesus Christ. She's nuts. I've only been to bloody Cardiff."

"*She said you left hours ago. I just got a bit worried.*"

"Everything's fine. I just stopped off at Ed's restaurant for a chat and then got something to eat. I'm only ten minutes away from home. I won't be long."

"There's no rush. Just wasn't sure where you were. I'll see you in a bit. Love you."

"Love you too. Bye." I hang up the phone and swallow the last of my Coke. Heading towards the doors, I spot an old friend sitting with his kids by the play-area. I go over to him and chat for another twenty minutes.

By the time I reach Swansea, my ass is in agony. Feel like I've been driving all day. The sun has started to go down already. Almost feels like winter for the day to disappear so quickly.

Pulling up outside the flat, I sit for a moment. The radio is off and the street is silent. Can't seem to move. Don't know what's wrong with me.

You know what's wrong.

You know damn-well.

You've been avoiding your own home all day.

Scared of a bloody ghost.

I shake off the ridiculous thoughts and unclip

141

my seatbelt. "Don't be so fucking stupid," I mutter to myself as I get out of the car. "I ain't scared of anything—especially a *fucking ghost*."

Slowly walking towards the building, I glance up at the flat. The kitchen light is on. I stop as I watch Aimee's shadow through the closed blinds. She doesn't need to know what happened last night— definitely this close to the wedding. The last thing I want is for her to freak out about nothing.

There is no ghost. No knocking on the door. It was a figment of my imagination. Nothing more. Or a well thought-out prank by someone. Maybe one of the guys. Probably Ed. Part of his best man speech.

Yeah that's it.

I open the main door and head inside. I hit the light switch on faster than usual and make my way up the stairs. Reaching the top, I suddenly feel a cold, creeping sensation all over my skin. I know it's nothing. I know it's just the sight of our door and the memory of that horrid knocking. Sighing loudly, I put it to the back of my mind, pull out my keys and open the door.

"My God," Aimee says as I enter the flat, "you

took your time. Thought you said you'd be ten minutes."

"I know, Sorry, Aim," I reply, closing the door behind and then putting on the chain. "I saw an old friend from school in Burger-Land. We just got chatting. You don't mind, do you?"

Aimee smiles. "Of course I don't mind. We're not joined at the hip. I was only curious."

I nod and follow her into the living room. "How was work?" I ask.

"It was all right. Pretty dead most of the day. You?"

We both sit on the couch.

"It was all right. Thought I'd go see Mum before the wedding."

"She's down in a few days for the rehearsal though. What was the point?"

"No point really. Just thought I'd go up for a chat, you know. Everything'll be a bit hectic in the rehearsal, what with your parents and Ed being there."

Aimee smiles tightly, a spark of distrust in her eyes. *She doesn't believe me.*

But there's nothing to hide. I did just go up to Cardiff to see Mum. And I did pop in to see Ed on the way. I haven't lied about anything.

So why the hell do I feel so guilty?

"How's your Mum?" Aimee asks. "Stressing about the wedding?"

"Yeah. You know my mother—always worried about something. She probably thinks Mexico is Colombia."

"It's a generation thing. My Dad's the same. He used to think that New Zealand was the capital of Australia."

"Piss off?" I chuckle. "That's awful. I thought your Dad was intelligent."

"He makes out that he knows everything. Likes to think of himself as a man of the world, but really he's just a narrow-minded dinosaur. He told me the other day that there are more gays and paedos in the world than ever before. Mum and me kept screaming at him to hear sense, that it's just that gay people don't need to hide like they used to, and police are able to catch more paedos. But did he listen? Like hell he did."

I shake my head in false-disbelief, too embarrassed to admit that I thought exactly the same. "Well, that's parents for you." I grab the remote control and turn on the TV. "You eaten yet?"

"Only a sandwich. Nothing big. Wanna make sure I fit into my wedding dress. Can't risk putting on weight this close."

"You look fine, Aim. Don't know why you're so stressed about your weight."

"I'm not stressed. But you can't be too careful. The dress is already a bit snug on me."

"Well, I don't care what you look like, Aim. As long as you turn up...I'm happy."

"That's good to know. But I'm sure my mother'll have something to say if I walk down the aisle in a pair of joggers and no makeup."

"Well I wouldn't."

Aimee smiles and kisses me.

"Shall we watch a film?" I suggest.

Aimee nods. "Could do. Not a long one though. Need an early night. I was knackered getting up for work this morning."

"That's fine. I could use an early night as well."

We select a DVD and sit back to watch. Snuggling up close to Aimee, I focus on the film. So glad she picked *Legally Blonde* and not some horror. Normally I hate that kind of shit—but tonight, I'll gladly settle for anything other than some creepy movie.

But even watching something so colourful and harmless I can still hear the knocking on the door. Can't get the sound out of my head, like some annoying pop song. Over and over it goes, through my mind, almost muting the sound of the TV. I fight hard to shake it off; I even force out a laugh when Aimee does. But it's no use. It's so loud I want to cover both ears. But that will only isolate the noise. I want to ask Aimee to turn the TV up, but she'll wonder what the hell is wrong with me. I want us to go to bed, to sleep through it, and wake in the morning, but I know I won't sleep. I want to ditch this cursed flat, find some other shoebox to live in—but we just can't afford anywhere else.

And anyway, that means it's won. *It's beaten us.*

And I won't let some *ghost* evict me from my

146

own home.

So fuck you ghost!

TEN

An hour with our parents and we're both bedbound. The rehearsal went pretty well, but definitely too much family for one day. We're lying side by side on the bed, staring up at the ceiling, dazed. I hold Aimee's hand and gently squeeze it. Turning to me, she smiles, and then kisses me on the lips.

"I can't wait for the wedding," Aimee tells me, her face just a few inches from mine. "But at the same time I'll be glad when it's over. Does that sound weird to you?"

I shake my head. "No. Not at all. I feel exactly the same way. It's our parents; they make things so complicated. It's just a bloody wedding for Christ's sake. People have been getting married for centuries. It shouldn't be this stressful."

"I know," she replies with an exaggerated sigh. "And Mum and Dad really did my head in today. Moaning about the table-gifts. What's wrong with giving everyone a lottery ticket? I don't think it's a stupid idea at all. Jesus, every wedding I've ever *been*

148

to they've given a box of sweets, or a miniature bottle of whiskey. But you're at a wedding—there's already booze there. What's the point? And sweets? That's even worse. It's not a children's party. At least lottery tickets are useful. Everyone likes lottery tickets—but not everyone likes whiskey and sweets."

"Imagine if one of our guests wins the jackpot," I say with excitement. "Do you think they'll split it with us?"

Aimee shrugs. "Not sure. Depends who wins. Don't think *I'd* split it with anyone. Not unless we won ten million. Would you?"

"Maybe give them a few quid, just for the sake of Karma. Best not to be too greedy."

I pull Aimee close and we cuddle.

"Right," Aimee says, wriggling free from my hold over her, "I've got work to do."

"What work?"

She gets up off the bed, drops to one knee, and then slides out a large plastic box from under the bed. "The lottery tickets. I've got to put them in gift-boxes."

Sitting up, hands behind my head, I tut. "Can't you do that tomorrow?"

She picks up the heavy box and puts it on the bed. "I won't have time tomorrow. I've got the hairdressers in the afternoon."

"Thought you said that some woman is doing your hair for the wedding."

"Yeah. But she's just putting my hair up for the wedding. I'm just going for a trim tomorrow. I told you this already." She starts to pull out tiny, white gift boxes, no bigger than a ring box, and then lays them out neatly on the quilt. "You never listen to me, Matt."

"Sorry, Aimee, that priceless nugget of information must have slipped me by."

"Smart arse," she retorts, not even looking at me; too engrossed in her task at hand.

Reaching into the plastic box, I pick out a huge bunch of lottery tickets, held tightly together with a rubber band. "How many tickets did you buy?"

"Fifty three. Someone's bound to win something."

"Why don't we just throw in a few jelly-babies

and keep the tickets for ourselves. We could use the money."

Aimee looks up at me and rolls her eyes. "Haven't you got something else you could be doing—instead of bugging me?"

"No. Nothing at all. Just annoy you."

Aimee pulls out a pair of scissors from the box and hands them to me. "Look, if you've got nothing better to do, then you can help me instead."

I moan, too exhausted even to pretend to want to help. "Do I have to? I need a shower."

"You just said you had nothing to do."

"Yeah, but that was before you actually *had* something for me to do."

Moaning even louder, I take the scissors by the handles and snip the air several times. "All right, what do you want me to do?"

She passes me some thin pink strips of ribbon. "Just pinch the ribbon with the scissors and pull, like you would on a balloon. You know, to make them curly."

I nod confidently, as if I'd done this a million times. "No problem. Watch an expert at work."

Aimee rolls her eyes again and watches as I attempt to curl the ribbon. Squeezing the scissors too tightly, the ribbon cuts in half.

"You're being too rough," Aimee says, taking the ribbon and scissors from me. "Let *me* do it."

"So what else can I do to help?"

"How about you clean the kitchen?"

"I meant with the wedding."

Aimee smiles, and then taps me on the leg. "In other words, I want you out of my hair." She air-snips the scissors playfully, and then motions for me to leave. "Go on, run along and let me get on with this. You'll only end up distracting me.

"Fine," I reply, getting off the bed. "But when your mother sees how shit your ribbons look, don't come crying to me."

Chuckling, Aimee shakes her head. "Yeah, like *that's* going to happen."

I leave the bedroom and head for the kitchen. For the first time ever, doing the dishes feels like a much better deal.

ELEVEN

I wake to the sound of screaming.

My head shoots up from the pillow in fright. Aimee is sitting up in bed, both hands on her head.

"What's wrong?" I ask her, my words filled with panic.

She moves her hands away from her head and turns to me, eyes drowning in tears.

It takes me a second to register—*but then I see it.*

The left side of her hair has been cut off.

My stomach roils when I see all the loose hair scattered on the pillow, quilt and bed sheets.

"*What the fuck!*" I mutter; too shocked even to console her.

Aimee leaps out of bed, hysterically. "We're leaving!" she screams, throwing a handful of hair at the wall.

"Calm down, Aimee," I say, following her out of bed. "Tell me what happened?"

"*You know exactly what happened, Matt,*" she sobs, storming towards the door. "*This fucking ghost cut my hair!*"

"Wait!" I shout, chasing after her. I grab her hand, but she slips from my grasp. "Just think about this for a second."

"*What's there to think about?*" she says as she races into the kitchen to grab the car-keys, and then Luna from the living room. "We need to leave now!"

Before I can even think of a reason for us to stay, Aimee is out the flat door.

"Wait!" I shout as I follow her downstairs and out of the building.

Outside is still dark, and I have no idea what the time is; my watch and phone are still up in the flat. So is my wallet.

Aimee races over to the driver's side of her car. "I'll drive," I demand.

She doesn't argue, just hands me her keys and climbs into the passenger side. I start the car and speed off down the street—with no clue where we're going.

The car is silent, apart from Aimee's shallow breathing. I glance over at her; her eyes are wide with madness, fixed to the road ahead, her right hand is stroking Luna as he sits on her lap, and her left hand is prodding and pulling at her ruined hair.

I look at the road again, struggling to process the situation. Did a ghost really cut her hair? Is that even possible?

A cold, gut-wrenching thought slithers through my mind—what if Aimee's face was cut instead?

Or her throat?

I quickly throw the notion to the back of my head, and focus on the road.

After a few more miles, Aimee finally speaks: "I think we should postpone the wedding."

Did I really just hear that? "What are you talking about?" I ask, stopping the car at the side of the road. "We can't postpone the wedding. It's too late. I've got family travelling all the way over from Ireland. And everything's paid for. The dress. The photographer. The whole lot."

"I don't give a shit! I can't walk down the aisle looking like this. Look at me!" She grabs the left side of her hair, parading the damage. "*It's ruined!* There's no way I'm showing my face until it's grown back. *No fucking way!*"

155

Reaching out, I try to take her hand, but she pulls away. "Look, why don't we drive over to your parents' house," I say, trying to appear composed, "take a minute to calm down, and think of a way to sort this mess out."

"There's nothing to sort out, Matt," she replies, sternly, wiping her eyes with her pyjama sleeve, "the wedding is off!"

I don't know what to say. My throat is dry, too shell-shocked to think of a simple resolution.

Maybe there isn't one.

I start to drive again, heading for Aimee's parents' house, squeezing the steering wheel in frustration.

Fuck this shit! There's always a solution.

It's time we found some help.

TWELVE

The thought of being driven out of my own home is ludicrous, especially by a ghost.

But all that ends today.

No more running, no more hiding, just a plan of action. And with every shitty situation, there's always a remedy.

And his name is Dylan Strong.

Finding a medium was pretty easy. Aimee's mother got his name from a friend, so I did a little research online, and Dylan's name kept popping up in various paranormal forums and articles. I checked out his website, read his many glowing testimonials, booked an appointment, and just like that this chubby, balding middle-aged man is now sitting on our armchair, dressed in a thick brown suit and yellow tie, sipping a cup of tea.

Aimee is sitting uneasily next to me on the couch, baseball cap on her head, grasping my hand tightly. I told her to stay at her parents' house, but she insisted, told me that I'd only mess it up if I saw

Dylan on my own. *Mess it up?* It's not like we've ever hired a medium before, so God knows why she'd think that.

"You say all this started when you first moved in?" Dylan asks, setting his cup down on the coffee table.

"Yeah, that's right," Aimee replies. "On our first day actually."

I turn to her with a frown. "I don't know about that, Aim."

"*Yes it did*," she barks at me defensively, like I've just accused her of lying. "The jar of beetroot smashed over the kitchen floor."

"Yeah, I remember, but we can't be sure whether that was just an accident."

"Tell me what else happened?" Dylan asks, clearly trying to move past our squabble. "No matter how small, because, when it comes to spirits, it's not always about the big events, the loud noises. Sometimes it's the little things, the tiny whispers, the cold chills; those are the first things to get under your skin."

"Well, there has been a strange draught in the

flat," I say, "but I assumed it was some hole in the wall, or a dodgy window."

Dylan picks up his tea and takes another sip. "And it absolutely could *still* be a draught coming from a window. I'm not going to sit here and tell you that everything you've experienced is a paranormal. That would be irresponsible of me. But when unexplained occurrences keep building up, then it's only right that we start thinking outside the box."

"Okay, then," Aimee continues, "next was my new mirror cracking. All my ornamental dolphins were smashed. The TV was pushed over. I saw a dark-haired woman in the bathroom, and Matt saw her again in the bedroom. And then," Aimee removes her baseball cap and shows Dylan her hair, "this happened."

Setting his cup down, he leans in closer to inspect. "Oh, I see. What happened there then?"

She slips the cap back on, and takes a moment to collect herself, squeezing my hand even tighter. As soon as she opens her mouth to speak, her first word brings on a bout of tears. I pull her into my shoulder, wrapping my arm around her.

"Three days ago," I cut in, "Aimee was using the scissors to decorate the wedding gift-boxes. When we woke up, her hair was like that."

Dylan's eyes broaden. "I see. And do either of you have a history of sleep walking, or any other sleeping disorders?"

Aimee and I shake our heads in unison.

Dylan reaches into his jacket pocket and pulls out a pair of glasses. He slips them on and then reaches into his leather satchel, which is positioned at the side of the armchair. He pulls out a black electronic device, about the size and look of a mid-nineties mobile phone, complete with a small silver aerial at the top. "Okay," he says, standing heavily with a groan. "I'll get started then."

"What does that do?" I ask as he turns the device on, its tiny screen lighting up blue. "Looks like something a Ghostbuster would have."

"This is an Electromagnetic Field Detector," he replies. "I use it to scan homes, making sure that magnetic fields aren't the cause of these occurrences."

"Sounds pretty technical," I say, as he walks around the living room, with the device pointing in front of him. "What do you need us to do?"

"Nothing for now, thank you," he replies. "I can find my own way round the flat."

Dylan exits the living room, with the device pointed straight ahead. He disappears into the kitchen, then the bathroom, points the device up at the hallway ceiling, opens the flat door, points it out onto the landing, and then finally enters our bedroom.

I imagine Dylan storming out onto the hallway, and then bursting out through the front door, his screams of horror fading as he flees the building. But I can also see a vision of him laughing at us, telling us that we're a pair of fucking morons for wasting his time with this bullshit.

After a few minutes, he emerges from the bedroom and then re-joins us in the living room.

"Well," Aimee says, "what does that machine say?"

Dylan's eyes scan each corner of the room, a deep grimace of concentration on his brow. "I'm not getting any readings," he replies, shaking his head. He then turns the device off.

"Does that mean that we definitely have a ghost then?" she asks.

Dylan sits down on the armchair. "I'm not picking up any spirits either. Not one."

"What?" she blurts out. "There must be something here."

He takes his glasses off and slips them back into his jacket pocket. "Normally when there's a spirit in a house, I feel something the moment I step inside. But," he shakes his head again, "there's nothing here."

"So what does that mean?" I ask, a tone of frustration in my voice. "Do you think we're making all this up?"

"No, of course I don't," he replies, waving his hand in protest. "If there *was* a ghost here, then it could have quite easily just left of its own accord."

"Really?" I reply with a frown of pessimism. "Just like that?"

"Absolutely, Matthew," he replies. "Remember—ghosts were once just like us. They would have loved, hated, laughed, felt remorse. The stress caused by cutting your hair could well have driven it away. Guilt can be a powerful thing."

Aimee lets out a stressed out sigh. "Okay, then—but what's to stop it coming back, though?"

"Well, that's the easy part," Dylan replies with a smile, and then reaches into his satchel again. "We cleanse your home." He pulls out a small white bowl and a bundle of light brown leaves, wrapped in string.

"What's that?" I ask, leaning forward to take a closer look.

"Sage," he replies, reaching into his jacket pocket. He takes out a blue lighter, ignites the end of the bundle, and then rests it in the bowl. "Hopefully this should keep your unwanted guest away."

As Dylan walks around the living room, with a bowl of burning sage held in front of him, I can't help but think that this is complete and utter drivel. Does all this really work? I glance at Aimee; her eyes are following him around, clearly intrigued.

"Are you sure there's nothing we can do to

help?" Aimee asks.

"Lots of positive energy from now on," he replies. "No fighting. No shouting. Just make your home into a nice, calming environment."

Aimee and I look at each other and grin, as if to say that selling the flat will probably be easier.

"Your mother tells me that you're getting married in a few days," he says to Aimee. "That's good—*very good*. Positive energy. Keep thinking it. You'll be surprised at how effective it is when dealing with a presence. Some of them feed off negativity."

We glance at each other again, this time with a look of guilt. I think about telling him that Aimee has called the wedding off, but there's no point.

Just as Dylan steps out of the living room, he says, "*oh*, and make sure your home is spotless. A clean house—positive energy. Trust me on that one."

Just as he disappears into the kitchen, I spot a few crumbs on the carpet, and dust on the windowsill.

Clean house? No arguing?

This is going to be tougher than I thought.

* * *

Dylan has finished his tea, taken his bag of ghost-repellents, and left Aimee and me alone in the flat. I can tell that she's still uneasy about being here; her body is hunched, her arms are crossed, and her eyes are constantly travelling around the living room. But it's daytime. Nothing seems as scary when the sun is shining.

"So what do you think?" I ask, struggling to hide my scepticism.

Aimee shrugs and then looks at me, her eyes broader than usual. "I don't know. He seemed like the real deal, and I have heard about burning sage before."

"So does that mean we can come home?"

Aimee's eyes inspect the room again. "Maybe," she replies with another shrug.

"How about we both stay away until after the honeymoon? You know, to give the place a good airing."

Letting out a long, tired exhale, she turns to me. "I don't know, Matt," she replies, taking her hat off again. "I just don't think I can face all those people with this mess on my head. *It looks vile.*"

I take her hand. "We need to do this, Aim. Positive energy, remember. If we postpone it, then all we're doing is letting it win, letting negativity rule our lives. This is our flat and our wedding, and we shouldn't be afraid in our own home. So let's show this *bitch* that nothing is going to drive a wedge between us."

Aimee starts to play with her hair in silence. She looks over at the sage on the coffee table, still burning in the bowl. "You're right," she says with a self-assured nod. "It's only hair—and there's always extensions." She smiles. "Let's do it."

Beaming, I lean forward and hug her. "Oh that's great, Aim." I come out of the hug and kiss her on the lips. "I love you so much."

"I love you too."

The relief that's surging through me is almost too much to bear. I want to scream it from the window, tell the world that I'm marrying the most wonderful person in the world. Everything that I've been through in my life, all the shit, all the misery, everything has lead me to Aimee.

And our ghost can kiss my fucking arse—*because I'm getting married!*

THIRTEEN

My wedding day. It's finally here.

Thank God for that.

Not just because of Aimee's hair, but the simple fact that I never thought I'd actually do it. I always thought that marriage was for parents and boring couples. I never truly believed that someone like me could ever be part of that dream. That fantasy of a normal life, with a normal woman. Maybe even have a kid down the road. Hell, maybe even two.

Definitely not three.

I massage my lower back with my thumb. It's still a little sore from sleeping on Ed's couch. I wonder how Aimee slept. Not too well I bet. Stressed about everything—especially her hair.

It's been raining for the last hour, but the news said that it would clear by ten. It's now five to eleven and it's not letting up. I'm trying not to let it bring me down. I was already expecting it to rain, even when I asked her to marry me. It's Britain after all. If I wanted guaranteed warm weather in summer, we should have got married abroad.

My ushers, Paul, Jones, and Mark, are busy handing out hymn sheets and guiding people to their pews. Ed is sitting next to me in the front row, reading from a crumpled up piece of paper, most definitely his speech. I scan the rest of the church in awe. So glad Aimee insisted on a church wedding. At the time it didn't seem important, especially since neither of us are religious. But now, staring at the breath-taking high ceilings, with its thick wooden beams, and the massive hanging cross just above the podium, it's obvious that we made the right choice. It's a gothic, stunning place that won't be easy to forget. There are about fifteen rows of pews, separated by a paved aisle. Mum is sitting behind me, chatting to Auntie Thelma, and on the bride's side, I notice Aimee's Mum, turned in her seat, eyes fixed nervously on the doors, clearly waiting for her daughter's grand-entrance.

My hands are trembling. I take a few deep breaths and they settle. "You've got the ring safe?" I whisper to Ed. "You better not have lost it."

Ed pats his top suit pocket and nods. "Stop

asking. You're making me paranoid."

"Can you blame me?"

"Look, I may not be the most reliable bloke in the world, but when was the last time I lost someone's wedding ring?"

"You've never been best man before."

"Exactly. So stop worrying, and just relax."

I nod, take another deep breath, and then pick up the hymn sheet. It's a four-page booklet, which Aimee made last week. Not something I could ever help with. It's not like she'd need my advice on which flowered pattern to have on the front cover.

Suddenly the room vibrates with movement as the old lady sitting at the organ behind the Reverend starts to play *The Wedding March* theme, and everyone's attention turns to the entrance. As Ed and I both stand, the double doors are pushed wide open. Jordan, Aimee's eight-year old niece, enters, dressed in light pink. Next to her is Aimee's older, slightly plumper sister, Nia, also in a light pink bridesmaid dress; her thick blonde hair pinned up high. Both girls are throwing flower petals on the floor as they walk.

And then I see Aimee.

I watch her, eyes glued as she makes her way down the aisle, escorted proudly by her father. She looks incredible with her white corset-style dress, clinging to her body, with the bottom-half dragging slowly behind. There's a lump in my throat. But it's not just because of the excitement I can feel exploding inside—it's the fact that I'm here, I've made it. I've found someone. Someone that loves me.

And it feels pretty fucking good.

Nudging me, Ed smiles when she's almost here; his eyes wide with unspoken envy. That's really something for him.

Aimee is now by my side. I don't notice her hair; I'm too drawn to her deep blue eyes, glowing like the first day we met; her smile that seems to be fighting off her tears. My hand is shaking again when I take hers. I whisper that she looks beautiful. She thanks me and we turn to the Reverend.

The vows feel like a dream. I repeat the words, we laugh when Aimee stumbles on hers, and then like no time has passed at all, I hear the words:

"I now pronounce you, husband and wife. You may kiss the bride."

* * *

"So how long before you two have kids?" Susanna shouts over the music; one of Aimee's drunken aunties; her heavy arm wrapped around me; her whiskey-smelling breath buried in my left ear. "Can't leave it too long. Neither of you is getting any younger. It's time to give up all that partying and get to it."

Smiling awkwardly at her, I spot Paul coming towards me. I throw him a pair of 'save me' eyes, and he comes over. "This is my good friend Paul." I tell her. Susanna is at least fifty, but she's single, and kind of loose. And Paul is thirty-three and will fuck anything that breathes. So there's a good chance that he'll take her off my hands.

She pulls away from my ringing eardrum and shakes his hand. "So you're Matt's friend then."

"Yep, that's me," Paul replies, his words slurry. "And you're one of Aimee's family?"

Susanna nods, her eyes half-shut. "I'm her auntie. Well, I suppose I can call her my friend now. She's old enough."

"Who's old enough," I hear Aimee say from behind my shoulder. "You better not be talking about me, Sue."

Susanna laughs. "There she is. There's my beautiful niece." Shoving past both Paul and me, she gives Aimee a big hug. Aimee has to practically hold the weight of her auntie up as she wraps her arms around her.

"I love you too, Sue," Aimee tells her; giving me a look to suggest that Susanna always gets like this.

Susanna then takes Aimee's hands, and looks deep into her eyes. "I'm so proud of you, honey. We all are. You've grown into such a wonderful person. You really have." She turns to me and takes my hand, dragging me next to Aimee. "And this boy here," she yanks my hand up to her mouth and kisses it, "this one's a *keeper*. Much better than that other boy. What was his name now? Steve? Or Stuart? Or Peter? What was it now, Aimee?"

Aimee rolls her eyes, but still with a smile on her

face. "It was Sam."

"That's the one. *Sam*. What a dickhead." She turns to me and kisses my hand again. "You've got nothing to worry about, Matt. That little *prick's* got nothing on you." She lets go of my hand and pinches my cheek playfully. "No one could compete with *this* handsome face."

Slightly annoyed by how hard she pinches me, I carry on grinning regardless.

"Leave them alone, Sue," I hear Aimee's father, Byron say as he approaches us, a pint of a beer in his left hand, and a disposable camera in the other. "You're slobbering all over them."

"I'm not slobbering," she replies, turning to her older brother, "I'm just showing some affection to these two lovebirds. Nothing wrong with that, is there?"

Ignoring his sister's question, Byron sets his glass down on a table, and then brings the camera up to his eye. "Everyone get in close," he nudges Paul with his hip. "You too, Paul. Get in there. Nice and tight now."

I wrap one arm over Aimee's shoulder, and the

174

other over Susanna's, and Paul squeezes in just front of me, ducking down a little.

Clearly just as drunk as his sister, Byron pushes the button at the top of the camera, but nothing happens.

"You need to wind it, Dad," Aimee shouts over to him.

Byron obeys his daughter, and tries again. "Big smiles now. Ready? Say cheese!"

"*CHEEEEEESE!*"

FOURTEEN

Nearly two months have passed since getting back from Mexico, and still nothing. No knocking at the door. No mirrors cracking. No TVs breaking. And no cold breeze in the middle of the day.

It's almost as if we both dreamed it all up.

Dylan Strong, you're a fucking legend.

Aimee and I are watching some programme about bugs. There's nothing else on so I'm enduring it.

She turns to face me on the couch; a massive, excited grin spread across her face, stroking Luna on her lap like a Bond-villain. I bet she's got one of her secrets to confess.

"Go on then," I say to her, rolling my eyes as I mute the TV. "What's the gossip?"

Aimee shrugs. "What gossip? Who said I had gossip?"

"*You did*—with that look you're giving me."

"Well, maybe I won't tell you now," she replies, her tone childlike. But it's obvious that it's only a matter of time before she does.

"Fine," I say, putting the volume back up, attempting to call her bluff. "I'm sure it's not important."

She prods me with her elbow. "You're a dick, Matt. For all you know I'm about to tell you that we've won the lottery."

I pick up the remote again but this time I turn the TV off. "Come on then. What's the gossip?"

She pauses as if about to hold it back, but then gives in almost immediately. "Well, do you remember Sarah from work?" she asks, prompting me to know exactly where this is going and how *un*-juicy this gossip will be.

"*Yeah*—the fat one?"

"She's not *fat*. She's just curvy."

"Okay: the curvy one then. What about her?"

"*Well*, yesterday she announced to everyone in the office that she's three months pregnant. And she's having twins!"

I pull off one of my best fake 'surprised' looks, and smile. I know I'm being a bit of an arse, but sometimes it's unavoidable, despite my best efforts.

177

"That's great news…for her."

"You don't think that's at all interesting?" Aimee asks, clearly annoyed by my lack of enthusiasm.

"Well, it might be great for her, but I don't even know the girl. So it's pretty hard to get excited about a stranger's good fortune." I pick up the remote control and put the TV back on. "But give her my love when you see her. Okay?"

Aimee goes silent. She's pissed off. I can feel it. I prefer it when she's screaming at me. Silence is never good. Turning to her, expecting to find her carrying a deep, resentful scowl on her face, instead I see a huge grin across her mouth. "What's so funny?" I ask, genuinely baffled. "I thought you'd be pissed off with me."

Aimee doesn't reply.

But then she says, "Sarah's not the only one who's pregnant."

Suddenly my jaw literally drops like a cartoon character. "What are you talking about?"

"What do you *think* I mean, dumbass? We're gonna have a baby as well."

"Are you serious?" I ask with a wide stare.

Aimee simply nods, eyes clearly swimming with elation.

"A baby?"

She nods again. "*Yep*. You and me are having a baby."

"Oh my god! That's awesome! That's...you better not be winding me up now. I mean..."

"'Course I'm not winding you up." Aimee takes hold of my hand. "We really are having a baby!"

I pull her close, kiss her on the lips, and then hug her tightly. "I love you so much," I tell her. "I'm so happy. I think this might be the greatest news I've ever had."

"Really?"

"*Damn right it is*. Even better than finding out about your fat friend."

Aimee laughs out loud. "Piss off. She's curvy."

Sitting back on the couch, I take a breath to absorb the news. I run both sets of fingers through my hair, and then turn back to Aimee. "How far gone are you? Do you know?"

"I think I'm about four or five weeks. Hard to tell with me; my periods are always all over the place."

"That sounds disgusting."

She lightly elbows me again. "What do you mean?"

"Doesn't matter."

"Well, I'll give the doctor a call tomorrow," Aimee continues, "to see about getting me a midwife. She'll probably have a better idea when I'll be due. But either way, we're looking at about June, July. Somewhere 'round there."

"That's even better news. A summer birthday. Nothing worse than one in January or December. Who the hell wants a birthday so close to Christmas."

"I think we've got a *few* years before we need to worry about that."

I still can't quite wrap my head around how exciting all this is. I mean, we've talked about having kids, but we've never actually planned it. I thought I'd be a little more terrified, but I'm not in the slightest. I'm thrilled! I couldn't be happier!

"I can't wait to tell Mum," I say like an excited child who's just won his first race.

"We can tell them this weekend if you like. We don't have to wait for the midwife."

"So when did you take the test?"

"This morning, before work. I wanted to be sure before I told you. Really wasn't expecting a positive, especially after being on the pill for so long."

"What if the test is wrong? Wouldn't it be safer to wait until we've seen a doctor?"

"No, it's fine. I've already done two tests. And besides, if the test says it's positive, then it's positive. It's when it says it's negative there could be an error. It might say you're not pregnant and then nine months later out pops a kid."

"Ah right. Okay. Let's tell your parents on Saturday. We can tell my mother when we see her for Sunday lunch. What do you think?"

"Yeah. Sounds like a plan." She looks down at Luna. "How would you like a brother or sister to play with, boy?" she asks in a vomit-inducing, childlike voice.

I roll my eyes. "He's a cat, Aim. He doesn't give a shit."

She kisses him on his furry, white head. "Of

course he does."

* * *

Aimee is still sitting up in bed, reading a book on baby-names. She's called out at least twenty-five boy names, and easily fifty girl names. Well, I'm no mentalist, but that definitely sounds like she's leaning towards wanting a girl. Although when I ask which she'd prefer, she just tells me that she doesn't care, as long as it's healthy.

Bullshit. Everyone's got a preference.

"How about Lloyd?" Aimee asks me, even though she knows that I've been trying to sleep for the last hour. "Or Archie? No, we can't have that. *Archie Archer*. That's ridiculous."

"All good, Aim," I mumble. "Just write down the ones you like and I'll take a look tomorrow. First thing."

"Or Lucy? I quite like Lucy. No, too much like Lucifer. Maybe Lacy. I quite like that. No, it sounds like a South African saying: Lassie. What do you think, Matt?"

I ignore her. I don't like any of those names. I know she's excited, but I'm exhausted. Haven't the heart to tell her to shut up. Maybe if I keep quiet she'll get the message.

"A girl in school was called Freya. I've always liked that name. Or Eva's nice too."

Another thirty minutes pass before she puts the light off and I finally hear the book closing and dropping onto the floor with a thud. Aimee shuffles next to me, and then within a matter of seconds, I hear her breathing heavily, clearly fast asleep. Already? I don't know how she does it. I really don't.

I try to push out the horrid thought of having to work tomorrow, and face yet another boring and pointless meeting about staff lateness. I mean, what's the point? We already get docked if we clock-in late, so we already get punished. It's not like we're salaried and we're wasting the hospital's money. Having long meetings about lateness *is* wasting money. That's irony at its best.

After maybe ten minutes of trying to drop off, I surrender and open my eyes. For a moment the room is in complete darkness, even with the bedroom door still open, and the faint glow from the street-lamps. I can just about see the doorframe and the dresser. Definitely need a bigger place. It's way too small. Can't see us coping when the baby gets here. It'll be fine for the first couple of months, the baby'll be sleeping in here with us, but after that we'll need at least two bedrooms. Don't fancy ending up stuffed into one room like *Charlie Bucket*.

My eyes adjust to the darkness and I start to see the shelves and the ornaments, and the photo frame on the wall next to the door, the one from the wedding, just the two of us. I wanted the one with our friends and us, but she insisted. Not worth fighting over—they're both stunning pics. Especially with Aimee looking so beautiful, so perfect, so composed; not like me at all. I look over at Aimee as she sleeps soundly, and I smile with pride.

But then my smile dissolves when I see something black hovering over her body.

It's shaped like a person.

Gasping in fright, I clutch the quilt as its shadowy hands reach down at her, as if clawing at her face and chest.

What the fuck is it?

It's not real. It's just my eyes playing tricks. It's just a shadow of something else. It's just the darkness.

It's not a person. It can't be.

Eyes wide with terror, I follow the shadow as it slithers away from Aimee, creeping over the bed towards me. I can't speak as the ice-cold air rushes over my face, like winter breath. I can hear it hissing as it looms above me. With no face. With no eyes. Just blackness. Just gloom reaching for me. Whispering inaudible sounds.

It's getting closer.

I can't move.

Closer.

It's too much to bear.

And closer.

I shut my eyes.

And closer.

It's not real. It can't be real.

And…

"LEAVE US ALONE!" Aimee screams.

The cold air suddenly vanishes.

Then the bedroom door slams shut.

Aimee puts the bedside lamp on, half-lighting the room. Her eyes are filled with tears. She clasps my forearm tightly, her nails digging into my flesh. I don't feel the pain. It's seems irrelevant. Whatever was here has gone. We say nothing; both eyes just locked to the closed door. Too petrified to dare go out into the hallway. Aimee's breathing is erratic like mine, her grip on my arm still firm.

A lifetime passes before I feel her fingers loosen and her breathing start to slow. I let go of the quilt and take hold of her hand.

"*You saw it,*" Aimee whispers, turning to me, eyes wider than I've ever seen them before, her words clearly broken by fear. "*Didn't you? You saw it too? The shadow?*"

I nod slowly, squeezing her hand even tighter.

"*I didn't imagine it…did I?*" Aimee stammers.

"No. You didn't imagine. I saw it too."

"*It's come back. Hasn't it?*"

I say nothing, just nod again. Too lost for words.

"*It never left, did it?*" Aimee says as she begins to

sob. *"It's always been here, hasn't it? Waiting for us. Watching us while we sleep. It's never gonna leave."*

"I don't know," I reply with shallow breath. "Just get dressed. We're going."

Both of us scramble out of bed. Aimee switches on the bedroom light. I throw on a pair of jeans and a T-shirt; Aimee does the same. I grab my wallet from the chest of drawers and we walk slowly to the door.

"I think my car keys are in the kitchen somewhere," I say. "Where are yours?"

Aimee shakes her head. "I don't know. I think in one of my handbags. Or maybe my coat pocket."

Reaching for the handle, I notice my hand shaking, yet my fingers seem frozen solid. I look up at Aimee; she knows exactly what's stopping me opening the door—it's obvious. I push past the dread, grasp the handle, and slowly twist the knob. Just as I start to pull the door open, I hear a small ping sound, and the room suddenly turns to darkness.

"Jesus Christ, Matt!" Aimee yells in fright, grabbing my arm tightly. *"It's in here again!"*

I frantically try the light switch but nothing happens. "Don't worry, Aimee. Just stay close to me. Everything's going to be all right." *What the fuck do I know?*

Beads of sweat dripping down my forehead, I slowly tow Aimee out of the bedroom and into the dark hallway.

The flat is in darkness, apart from the dim light of the street-lamps, seeping through the living room curtains. I hit the hallway light switch but nothing happens. I can just about make out the wall and the photos on it. I see the flat door. Unhooking the chain, I open it, and then motion with my head for Aimee to go through it. "Run to my car," I whisper with urgency. "I'll get the car keys." She nods and then scurries out onto the landing and down the stairs, not sparing even a second to try the light switch.

And then she's out of sight.

Leaving the door to the flat wide open for a sharp exit, I stampede through the blackness into the kitchen. Futilely, I try the light switch again but nothing happens. The room is even darker than the rest of the flat. I feel about on the table for the keys. Covering most of the table, I can't find them. As my fingers give the table one last sweep, I knock the bunch of keys onto the floor. Following the rattle as they land, I reach down blindly and manage to gather them up.

A loud thud vibrates under my feet.

I bolt out of the kitchen only to find the flat door closed—and the door-chain hooked back on.

I gasp in horror.

Impossible.

It's not real.

As I unhook the chain, scrambling to turn the knob, a sudden gush of cold air hits the back of my neck, snaking around past my ears to both cheeks.

And then that slow, hissing sound creeps into my eardrums again, infesting my skin with goosebumps.

I can't breathe as it slides down over my throat.

I know she's there.

Behind me.

Watching.

Too frightened to face it, I burst through the

door. Across the landing. Down the stairs. Leaping the last five steps. And then I'm out of the building.

Relief washes over me as the cool night breeze hits me, and I see Aimee, standing nervously against the car. I open the car door and we scramble inside.

As we speed away down the street, towards the city centre, all I can think about is that vile shadow, hovering over Aimee, and that awful hissing sound.

I feel sick.

Muscles tight, sweat running down my forehead, I glance up at the rear-view mirror—but then quickly move it over to the left.

I don't want to see into the backseat. I've seen enough for one day.

Just as we reach the motorway, heading towards Aimee's parents' house, something hideous dawns on me.

We forgot the fucking cat!

FIFTEEN

We pull up outside the flat. It's started to rain, filling the sky with grey clouds, concealing the sun that was shining only twenty-minutes ago. The dark and gloomy weather doesn't exactly help our current situation.

I rub my tired eyes hard with my palms. I didn't get a wink of sleep last night. Neither did Aimee.

How the fuck could anyone sleep after all this shit?

Aimee unclips her seatbelt and grabs the door handle. I take her other hand, preventing her from opening it. "Stop," I tell her, firmly. "I told you to stay put. You can't risk the baby."

"Look, I was the one who forgot Luna—so I need to do this, Matt. He's my cat."

"No, Aimee," I reply, shaking my head in protest. "We both forgot him, so I'm going alone. I'll grab him, find your car keys, and then pack up our things. I'll be in and out in two minutes."

"I don't care!" She pulls her hand free from my grip and then opens the door. "I'm coming with you."

I sigh, and then reluctantly follow her out of the car. "*Fine*. But you stay next to me the whole time. Agreed?"

"Okay."

Walking up to the building, hand in hand, we both look up at the living-room window. Not sure what I'm looking at, what I expect to see. But this is not how someone should be entering their home—filled with worry and dread. Pulling out my keys, I fretfully open the door. The corridor light is somehow on. Aimee's grip on my hand tightens as we make our way up the stairs, each footstep somehow creaking louder than the last. At the top I notice the door to our flat still hanging wide open. Memories of the floating shadow come rushing back. I shake them off, take a breath, and then slowly step inside the flat. My heart is racing but I try to hide my anxiety. The last thing Aimee needs now is to see me in a state, especially in her condition.

"Luna!" Aimee calls out to him. "Come here, boy."

No response.

Heart racing, I enter the living room, followed closely behind by Aimee.

"Luna!" she calls out again, checking behind the couch and armchair. "Where are you boy?"

I glance behind the TV stand, but he's not there.

Aimee's car keys are on the coffee table. I pick them up and hand them over to her.

"Luna!" I yell as we head into the kitchen. "Come on you silly cat. Where are you?"

I check under the table and chairs. Deserted. Aimee inspects the rest of the room but he's still missing.

"Where the hell is he?" Aimee asks; her face gripped with unease.

"Don't worry. He's probably sleeping under our bed."

She leaves the kitchen before me, heading towards our bedroom. "Wait for me, Aimee!" I snap as I chase after her. "It's too risky."

Aimee stops suddenly just outside the bathroom door.

"What's wrong?" I ask as I peer inside over her

shoulder. My eyes are immediately drawn to the mirror above the sink, and the words scribbled in red lipstick, covering most of the glass. They're too hard to make out from here, so I follow her in for a closer look.

Jesus fucking Christ!

The words read: *'YOUR BABY IS MINE.'*

My insides start to constrict, robbing me of my breath.

I wish we'd stayed out of this room, ignored this *fucking mirror*—because when I see the bathtub, the torn clumps of white fur, now a dark pink colour, I realise that the words are not written in red lipstick.

"*Oh my God!*" Aimee cries, her hand over her mouth. "*Oh my fucking God! Luna!*"

Trying to mask my horror, I take hold of Aimee's right arm, and pull her away from the bathtub. "Don't look at him," I say, struggling not to vomit at the sight of Luna's severed abdomen, his spewing innards, the pool of dried blood under his motionless body. "We need to go."

Aimee starts to sob uncontrollably, the colour in her cheeks drained, her body juddering with shock.

Guiding her out of the bathroom, I catch another glimpse of the words scrawled on the mirror.

Somehow my stomach churns even more.

There's nothing left for us in this flat.

She can have it all.

Like zombies, we leave the building, and then climb into my car again. Struggling to catch my breath, I notice Aimee's car still parked in front. She's in no state to drive today. God knows what might happen.

I want to comfort her, tell her something to make everything better. But I can't. I've got nothing to say. Nothing at all to ease her pain, her worry.

To bring back Luna.

This thing drove us out into the night. It has driven us out of our home.

And now it wants our unborn child as well.

SIXTEEN

We haven't spoken properly since officially moving in with Aimee's parents. At first I put it down to working so many evening shifts at the hospital, the long commute, hardly seeing each other. But it's not just that, or even seeing Luna in such a vile way.

It's the words on the mirror.

I'm partly to blame for distancing myself from Aimee. It's been easy with Byron and Lynne as distractions. There's rarely a moment of awkward silence to fill, and I've told myself that it's best just to give her time, let her get over the stress. But I know it's just another one of my excuses not to face up to things. It's hard for me too, though. I saw the message. It's my baby as well. It freaked me out just as much. I'm the one who's meant to keep my wife safe, keep my family safe.

I can't even keep the fucking cat safe.

I took a bus back to the flat yesterday to pick up Aimee's car. I did contemplate just driving away, but instead I rushed up to the flat with a bin-bag, dropped Luna's remains inside, and then buried him by the reservoir.

I hated the little fur-ball, but no one deserves to die in such a way.

We still haven't told anyone that Aimee's pregnant—not even her parents. She told me that she'd like to wait a couple more weeks, at least until our first scan. But it seems like ages since the news; she's even started to show a little. I've noticed her wearing those loose-fitting blouses to cover up her stomach. Don't think her parents have noticed though. Personally I can't see the problem with telling them; they're going to find out sooner or later. And if she waits too long, our parents are going to wonder what took us so long. Plus, we could use the distraction. Giving everyone the great news is bound to take away some of those negative feelings. At least when we say that we want to sell the flat, we can use the baby as an excuse.

* * *

"So how's the flat coming along?" Byron asks me,

stuffing in a mouthful of chicken.

"Not really sure," I reply, as the memory of Luna's dead body pops into my head. "We're still waiting for *British Gas* to get back to us."

"Well I hope they're giving you a discount from next month's bill," Lynne says from the sink, scrubbing dishes with a brush. "It's not fair on you both, being turfed out like that. Make sure you tell them you're not happy."

"Stop badgering them, Lynne," Byron mumbles with a mouthful of food. "You make it sound like we don't want them here."

"I'm not saying that," Lynne replies. "I'm just saying that it's not fair. Especially with how far they have to travel to work every day."

"So how's work been treating you these days?" Byron asks Aimee. "Those lawyers still taking advantage of you?"

"No, Dad. It's fine," Aimee replies; her words quiet, not looking at her father, eyes staring down at her food.

"They've been really good with her lately," I answer, trying to move the focus back over to me.

"They've even booked her on one of those advanced computer courses."

"That's great news, Aimee," Lynne says to her, proudly. "'Bout time too."

Aimee nods and smiles thinly.

"Well, she deserves it," I say. "She's been there long enough."

"Damn right!" Byron says, reaching over the table to take a dollop of swede from the bowl.

There's an awkward silence for a few minutes, apart from the sound of cutlery scratching down on plates, and dishes being pulled out of the sink and stacked on the drainer.

"You're quiet, Aimee," Byron tells her. "You feeling all right? You've barely touched your food."

"I'm fine, Dad," she replies, prodding her lumpy mash potato with the fork. "I'm just not that hungry."

Lynne turns to her, her eyes filled with motherly concern. "It's not like you to waste so much food."

"It's nothing, Mum. Stop fussing," Aimee snaps, dropping her cutlery down onto the table. "There's nothing wrong with me. I'm just tired. That's all."

I watch as Byron is about to defend his wife, but then stops when he sees that Aimee is clearly upset. The kitchen falls quiet again for almost a full minute. It feels like a lifetime as I forcefully eat my meal, even though I've completely lost my appetite.

"Why don't you have a lie down upstairs?" I ask Aimee, breaking the silence. "I'll help Lynne clean up."

Aimee starts to cry. The chair screeches against the tiled floor as she pushes it back with her feet. Standing up, she mouths a barely recognisable apology, and rushes out of the kitchen. I nearly get up and go after her, but I stay put, let her cool off for a couple of minutes. I'm guessing that this isn't the first time that she's stormed out of this room. But this isn't some teenage tantrum; this is a real problem. I wish I could tell her parents the truth; that Luna didn't just run away, that a ghost drove us out of the flat—and that Aimee is pregnant. But she made me swear that I wouldn't. She doesn't want them to worry. So I'll bite my tongue—for now.

After helping Lynne with the dishes, I go upstairs to speak with Aimee.

I stand outside the bedroom door for a moment, listening to Aimee weep. I lightly knock on her bedroom door and then walk in. Aimee is lying on the bed, with her back to me, facing the window. Seeing her so distressed, so lost, makes my stomach tighten. I sit next to her, my hand stroking her soft hair. "It's going to be all right, Aim," I say quietly. "You know that, don't you?"

She doesn't answer, her body juddering as she sobs.

"Talk to me," I say. "Please."

There's a moment of silence, but then Aimee finally turns to face me. "There's nothing to say, Matt," she replies with red, tear-filled eyes. "I just can't believe what she did to Luna. And now we're—"

"What's that?" I ask, cutting her off when I notice the dark patch on the crotch of her jeans.

But the moment the words leave my lips, I know exactly what it is.

With a look of confusion, Aimee peers down at the stain. "*Oh shit,*" she mutters under her breath as her eyes widen in horror.

My heart sinks into my gut and I leap off the bed. "We need to get you to the hospital."

She nods, tears still streaming, and then grabs one of her long coats from the back of the door. She quickly slips it on, covering up the bloodstain, and then we race out of the bedroom.

She waits by the flat door as I walk into the kitchen to get the car keys. Byron has vanished somewhere, leaving just Lynne sweeping the floor. She smiles when she spots me. "Popping out somewhere?" she asks as I gather up the car keys from the damp worktop.

"Yeah, just a quick drive to clear Aimee's head. We won't be long."

"Is she all right?" she asks with suspicion; she's clearly noticed Aimee standing by the front door. She knows something's not right; it's pretty obvious. Maybe she thinks we've just had a falling out. But I doubt it. Mothers always know.

"Yeah, she's fine, Lynne," I reassure her, playing with my keys awkwardly, unable to make eye contact.

"Okay, *well*. . . I'll see you both later then."

"Okay, Lynne. See you later." I force a smile and leave the kitchen swiftly.

Aimee opens the front door even before I reach her. Catching up with her on the front path, I take her hand; it's rigid. I can tell she wants me to keep my distance. But I won't let her. By the time we get across the street to the car, I feel her fingers start to loosen. I stop her just before we get to the car door and pull her close; she resists at first, but then surrenders. I hug her tightly as she sobs wildly into my chest. I tell her that it'll be all right. Whatever happens. Whatever the outcome. I'll always be there for her. And I'll always love her more than anything.

SEVENTEEN

Summer is over.

And it feels like shit. That cold evening breeze, the light fading fast. But as a kid, the worst part was always the last week before we all went back to school after summer break. I could never appreciate that I still had a whole week left away from the place. For me, it always felt like one long, depressing Sunday, counting down the seconds before it was all over. Sunday was bath-night and dismal TV programmes. Nothing but crappy dramas and religion.

But things change. Sundays are great. TV is better, and bath-night is now shower night.

School just sucked arse.

Aimee said she loved school; that it never bothered her going back after summer. Not sure why. Maybe she just had more friends than me, was better at maths, kissed more teachers' arses. Who knows?

I wish I'd met her back then; it might have

saved me a shitload of teenage heartache. But back then I wouldn't have stood a chance with someone like her. Someone so popular. So beautiful.

And now I have her. The woman of my dreams. A woman that I would have given anything just to talk to; just to be near. But I can't seem to help her now. I can't stop her from crying. No matter what I tell her, nothing seems to seep through. It's as if she's just given up. My rational side is telling me to give her more time to get over losing the baby. It's only natural to feel down, disconnected.

But there's nothing natural about *any* of this.

Could a ghost have done this to her? Forced a miscarriage?

No—it's just a coincidence. Women have miscarriages every day. My mother has had three herself.

Aimee'll get over it; move on.

What if she doesn't, though?

What if she never wants another baby?

When I touch her, she pulls away. When I ask her if there's anything I can do, she tells me no. I can't ask her parents for help; they still don't know about the pregnancy. We've been hiding in her room for the past few days. I have a feeling that they've put two and two together and worked it out. They are her parents after all.

Yesterday evening, when Aimee had been sleeping all day, a good twenty hours, I was tempted to have a quiet word with Lynne. I even came down stairs, took her into the kitchen—but then I chickened out at the last second. I imagined sending Aimee even further into depression, placing an even deeper wedge between us. So I just asked Lynne if it was all right if we stayed a little longer while we tried to sell the flat.

Today has been particularly difficult. When I woke up this morning, I was certain that Aimee would start to show signs of pulling through, but as the day has gone on, and with no glimmer of her returning to work, that dream has now faded.

I've spent the last two hours, lying next to her, stroking her hair as we watch TV in bed. We haven't spoken for the duration of the film. Normally I'd insist on silence, but now it just feels awkward and sad.

I just want her back. I just want to see that smile again.

I keep telling Aimee that it just wasn't our time to have a baby; that it had nothing to do with the occurrences, the stress. But she can tell that I don't really believe it. She can see it in my eyes. I try to put on a brave face, pretend that everything will be all right, but I'm not so sure anymore. Maybe things won't be. Maybe this *is* the beginning of the end. A dark path that leads—

Shut up you dick!

What are you talking about?

This is nothing!

This is just a tiny little bump in the road!

What the hell's the matter with you?

Lots of couples go through this.

You're not the first to lose a baby—and you won't be the last.

I have to be strong for Aimee. She needs to look into my eyes and believe every word I say. Because I *will* get through this. We *will* have another baby.

And we *will* find a new place to live.

Ghost-free!

So stop your fucking whining!

EIGHTEEN

Finally a little good news—we've sold the flat.

It took us a while, lost a little money, had a few more sleepless nights over the moral implications, but in the end—what choice did we have? Live with a vengeful ghost? Pay a mortgage on an abandoned property?

Burn it to the ground?

Aimee and I pull up outside the third house on the list. 56 Cornel Road. The estate agent gave us eight possible properties to view, within our measly budget. We've scratched off four already. I didn't like the fact that most of them were by the train station.

This house is small, mid-terrace, with the front door stepping directly out onto the narrow pavement. The door is lime green. Aimee hates green, but we can always paint it. The neighbourhood seems quiet, apart from the sound of passing cars on the opposite street. And there's a pub just five doors down. Very convenient.

Not so great for Aimee.

"What do you think?" Aimee asks, pulling a face like she's just eaten something rotten. "I'm not too sure about being so close to a pub?"

"Depends what kind of pub it is. Might be one of those quiet little country pubs."

"Don't be ridiculous. We're nowhere near the countryside. It's more likely to be full of pissheads. God knows how loud the music will be."

"They can't have music too loud. It's in the middle of all these houses. There are laws against that."

Aimee sighs, scans the street up and down, and then takes my hand. "Come on then, let's check it out."

We walk up to the house. I ring the bell and within seconds the door opens. David the estate agent is standing in the porch, suit and tie on, big smiles, small stature. He can't be more than five feet tall, even shorter than Aimee's five-two frame. It's great—makes me feel like a giant.

"Good Morning, Mr and Mrs Archer," he says; his voice chirpier than anyone's should be at nine in the morning. "Find the place all right then?"

"Yeah, not too bad," Aimee replies. "It's not far from where I work. Only about half a mile."

David ushers us inside. "Well then, this might be a perfect little buy for you both. You'll save a fortune in fuel costs."

"It would be nice to walk in for a change. It's usually murder first thing." Aimee leads the way through the porch and into the living room. The room is big, which gives the impression that it's two rooms knocked into one. The staircase comes down into it, which means no hallway. I've never been sure about houses like this. I always thought that a hallway was essential. But looking at it, I kind of like it. It'll make parties much easier. Guests can use the living room, and drift in and out the kitchen. The room could use a lick of paint, but it's nice. Nice and square. Perfect to become my unofficial cinema-room.

"As you can see," David continues, "the walls and ceiling have been plastered. And the large window in the front is only two years old. In fact, apart from the kitchen, all the windows are double-glazed and only two years old, so at least you know that they're done, they're safe, and your insulation should be good throughout the winter."

"Yeah, that is good," I say, not really interested in the windows. More concerned with judging how big a TV I can get on the wall. Maybe even a projector.

Aimee'll kill me.

We inspect the two-bedroom house, from top to bottom, until finally David goes outside and gives us a little privacy to speak in the living room.

"Well," I say, "what do you think of the place?"

Aimee gives the room another scan. "Apart from the pub outside, I really like it."

I nod, grinning excitedly. "Yeah, me too— especially this room. I think it would be great for friends coming over. And I like the garden too. Not too big, but big enough to have a barbecue in the summer."

"You don't think having just concrete is gonna be a bit annoying?"

"No, not really. Neither of us is going to cut the grass anyway. At least it's easy to maintain."

"Are you sure about that?"

"Yeah. Of course I am. Why does it bother you so much? It's not as if you're into gardening."

Aimee walks over to the furthest window, which looks directly into the garden. She pushes the blinds to one side and stares out. "What if we end up having a baby? Where would they play?"

Hearing her speak so optimistically about our future, about trying for another baby, fills me with such warmth, such hope...*such relief.* I knew it was only a matter of time before she came around, before she saw sense again.

I'm desperate to talk more to her about trying again, but I don't. Instead, I put it to one side and focus on the house.

And our future.

"What about the pub?" I ask her.

"I know. That's the only thing that's putting a spanner in the works."

"Maybe we can ask the estate agent about it. See what he thinks."

"What's the point? He's not exactly going to tell us that it's a shithole. We'd be better off popping back in the night to see for ourselves. Maybe even asking next door."

I walk over to the window, taking Aimee by the hand. We both peer out into the garden. I picture the barbecue with sirloin steaks sizzling on top, a table beside it, stacked with bread rolls and ketchup. No salad. I see Ed, Jones, Paul, and the rest of the guys standing 'round it, laughing and joking, each holding a bottle of ice-cold beer. And then, just back a little, next to the wooden shed, I see a pink trampoline. There's a little girl bouncing high, about five-years old, big smile spread across her face, her long blonde curls bobbing up and down. And there's Aimee, watching from its edge, making sure the little girl doesn't fall off.

The child's face is too far away to make out. But I know she's beautiful. It's obvious. She looks like Aimee. My beautiful, perfect Aimee.

Outside the house, we're greeted by the estate agent, just finishing up on a phone call. "Well, what's the verdict then?" he asks; his voice clearly filled with eagerness and sanguinity. "Any thoughts?"

"Yeah, we like it," I reply. "We like it a lot. But there's just one problem."

"Oh, right. And what's that?"

"The pub down the road," Aimee cuts in. "I'm not so sure that I want to live so close to one. What with all the loud music and drunk people. Doesn't sound very appealing, especially if we have children."

The estate agent smiles. "Then you're in luck, Mrs Archer. It's a very quiet pub. It has to be. By law. It's just full of retired old men. It might get a little loud if there's a rugby match on, but most matches are shown in the afternoon, and people have usually moved on by six to the next pub. Honestly, it'll be fine. I mean, if you're worried, then it might be worth asking one of the neighbours what they think of the place."

"Okay," she replies, "we will."

"Can we have a think about it and get back to you?" Aimee asks David. "There are a few things we need to discuss. But we are interested. So…"

"Of course it's fine," he replies. "Take as long as you need. Buying a house is not something you should rush into. Take your time."

I shake David's hand. "Thanks. We'll be in touch. Probably later on today."

"No problem. I look forward to it."

Aimee also shakes his hand. "Thank you, David."

We watch as he drives off down the street, beeping his horn as he disappears around the corner.

Hand in hand, we take a step back and gaze at the house. Turning to Aimee, I smile, and then kiss her on the lips. "I love you," I tell her.

"I love you too."

I pull her close, arms wrapped around her waist, and then motion with my head towards the pub. "Fancy a quick pint?"

Aimee chuckles. "Bit early."

"Well...you better get used to it then."

NINETEEN

We spend most of Christmas Eve dragging furniture into the house. Byron said he'd help but he's put his back out again, and everyone else is either working or with their families. Luckily our new neighbour, Henry and his son Philip kindly offered to give us a hand with the heavy stuff. Thank God. Don't know how we would have finished before midnight.

Most of our things are either unpacked in their correct places, or still in boxes, scattered across the living-room floor. Normally Aimee would be on my case to finish up—but not today. We've been sat on this tiny couch for nearly an hour, staring at the wall where the TV should be. And normally that would be the first thing that was up and running, but I just can't find the strength.

I'm starving too. Haven't eaten since twelve this afternoon, and now it's going on eleven. Too tired even to eat. There's nothing here anyway, and the fridge won't be delivered until the New Year.

"I'm going to bed," Aimee announces. "I'm

knackered. You coming?"

Before I answer, I contemplate devouring the half-eaten bag of crisps from Aimee's handbag, the one that I spotted this morning. But I think I'll pass. God knows how long they've been in there. "Yeah. Why not. It's Christmas Day tomorrow. Need to get some sleep. We've got a busy day."

Aimee sighs dramatically. "Parents all day long. Just what I need."

Standing up from the couch, I grab Aimee's hand and pull her up. "Come on, lazy-bones, it'll be fine. We can't exactly spend Christmas Day here."

"Why not?"

"Because we haven't even got a microwave, let alone an oven. How are we supposed to cook a turkey?"

We make our way towards the stairs. "I don't care," she says, her words muffled by a yawn. "I'd be happy watching cheesy Christmas films all day, stuffing my face with chocolate and wine."

I chuckle as we walk up the stairs. "That does sound nice."

At the top, the dark, narrow landing fills me

with a feeling of foreboding.

"What's wrong?" Aimee asks.

"Nothing. I'm fine," I reply with a forced smile.

"Tell me. What's up?"

"Just weird living on our own again. That's all."

"Yeah. I know how you feel. If I'm being honest, I was dreading moving in today."

"Really?"

"Yeah, I was. But we've been so busy I almost forgot about everything."

"Yeah, me too. It's been a good distraction." We start to walk towards our bedroom. "I know it'll be fine. It's just…"

"I know, Matt. Let's just get some sleep and try not to dwell on it. We need to get on with our lives."

"You're right."

Once inside the bedroom, Aimee switches the light on. The room still has that horrid cream and brown flower-patterned wallpaper. *That's definitely going.* The light blue carpet is okay, just a little grubby. Aimee wants it changed though, and the only furniture we have in here is our bed, plonked down at the very centre of the room—without sheets, quilt or pillows. I groan loudly when I realise that they're still in one of the boxes downstairs. Aimee chuckles, then takes my hand and escorts me over to the bed. We both collapse onto the soft mattress, face down, eyes closed.

"Let's just lie here for a minute," Aimee drowsily says. "I'll nip down to get the quilt later."

"Sounds like a plan."

I wrap my arm around Aimee and pull her close. "I love you, Aims."

"I love you too."

We don't move an inch for maybe five or so minutes before I realise that I need a pee.

TWENTY

Summer's coming.

Paul has been seeing Aimee's sister, Nia for the past four months. I think it's awesome, but Aimee wasn't too happy at first. I don't blame her. We all know what Paul's like, and I think Aimee is more worried about her niece, Jordan. But who's to say what works. They're still together, and they seem happy enough. Let them get on with it I say. Being a stepdad might be exactly what Paul needs.

The night air is chilly, but warm enough to sit outside on our wooden picnic table. Aimee was good enough to bring me my black *Kasabian* hoodie, and a plain green one for Paul.

"We definitely need to go camping this year," Paul tells me, finishing the last of his beer bottle. "We haven't been for years."

"Yeah, I'd be up for that," I reply, enthusiastically. "Maybe down the Gower. Or Brecon. I'm sure Ed and the guys will fancy it."

"What about us then?" Nia asks, huddled close

to Paul, clearly feeling the cold. "Can't we come on your little camping trip?"

Paul turns to her. "Didn't think it would be something you girls would be in to."

"Oh really," Aimee cuts in, "and why's that?"

I can see the discomfort in Paul's eyes. This is his first *proper* relationship, so he has no idea that the girls are just teasing him. I happened to know Aimee and Nia *pretty well*, and I'd put money on it that neither of them would set foot in a bloody tent.

But it's fun to watch Paul suffer.

"Can't women enjoy the great outdoors?" Nia asks. "Or is it just reserved for big strong men?"

"And what about jobs?" Aimee asks. "Should we get paid the same as big strong men? *Oh*, and I suppose women are terrible drivers as well."

"I'm not saying that," Paul squirms. "I'm just saying that men are—"

"They're joking, Paul," I interrupt, before he digs an even bigger grave for himself. "These two can't stand camping. I've been trying to get Aimee to come for years. Don't listen to them."

Aimee elbows me softly in the ribs.

"Spoilsport."

"Don't be so boring, Matt," Nia tells me. "You know how gullible he is."

"*Hey*, what's that supposed to mean?" Paul asks, defensively, even though he's smiling. "I'm not gullible. I'm just too trusting, that's all."

"No mate," I say to him, taking a sip of beer, "you're just gullible."

Everyone laughs, including Paul. "Cheeky fucker," he says. "Picking on the bald guy, is it? You know, I bet Bruce Willis doesn't get *half* the shit that I get."

Nia kisses him on the cheek. "Yeah, but Bruce Willis is rich—*and* handsome."

Paul shakes his head, grinning, and gets up off his seat. "Right, I'm going for a piss. Does anyone need another beer? Mr Gullible-baldy-bastard will get it."

Still chuckling, I wave my hand in protest. "No thanks, mate. I'm good."

"How about you, Aimee?" he asks. "Surely you can have *one* beer. You'll be fine for work in the morning."

"Yeah, why can't you have a few?" Nia asks. "To Hell with those stuck-up bloody lawyers. It's not like they'll notice anyway."

"No, it's too risky driving that early," Aimee replies. "The police are more likely to pull you over on a Saturday morning. It's not worth it."

"Boring cow," Nia says. "*I'll* have another beer, Paul. In fact, raid their cupboards for a bottle of vodka. I'm sure they've got one stashed away somewhere."

Paul nods, his grin wide. "And I know where he keeps it."

"Fine," I say. "Bring it on. I'm up for some shots. We haven't really had a proper housewarming party anyway. So fuck it—let's get hammered."

"Cool," Paul says as he walks towards the house. Just at the backdoor, he stops, and then looks at me, and then at Aimee, grimacing hard, like Jessica Fletcher figuring out who killed the tennis coach. "Why do you need to be sober tomorrow? You can walk from here. You told Nia that your office was less than a mile away."

"Did I?" Aimee says guiltily, clearly fighting hard

not to laugh.

"Yeah, you did too," Nia says, turning to her sister. But then, as if someone had just whispered it into her ear, she excitedly blurts out: "You're pregnant!"

Aimee smirks, and then she nods her head.

"Oh my god! Congratulations, Sis!" Nia says, hugging her tightly. "I bloody knew there was something fishy going on. I knew you'd never say no to booze. Why didn't you tell me? How far gone? Come on, I need details. Every last one. Do Mum and Dad know yet?"

"Slow down, Nia," Aimee replies. "No one knows. Only us four. I was going to tell everyone this Sunday when we're over for lunch."

Paul shakes my hand and gives me a firm pat on the back. "That's awesome news, mate. Really chuffed for you." He then goes over to Aimee, reaches down and kisses her on the cheek. "So how far gone are you?"

"Three months," Aimee replies, rubbing her stomach proudly. "We had the scan this morning."

"And is everything okay?" Nia asks. "Everything

healthy?"

"Looks like it. So far anyway. Way too early to tell, but...fingers crossed."

I reach over the table and place my hand over Aimee's. She smiles at me. "We've been dying to tell people since we found out," I say. "But we didn't want to jinx it. You know?"

"Yeah, of course I do," Nia says. "You never know what could happen. The last thing you want to do is tell the world on Facebook, and then something happens and you have to tell everyone the bad news."

"All right, Nia," Paul says. "Let's not depress everyone."

"It's all right, Paul," Aimee says. "She's right. Anything can happen. But now I'm happy to tell everyone. I've been looking forward to it."

Paul gives me another pat on the back. "Right, I still need that piss, so when I get back—we're bloody celebrating. No excuses." He looks over at Aimee. "Except you of course. No shots for at least a year."

"Thanks for reminding me, Paul," Aimee sighs.

"I think I'll be pulling my hair out by then."

* * *

We wave Paul and Nia goodbye as their taxi pulls off down the street. I kiss Aimee on the lips, playfully spanking her arse as she goes back inside the house. I follow her, closing the front door behind me.

Aimee sits on the couch, groaning loudly, as if she's just finished one of her twelve-hour shifts. "Jesus Christ, I'm so tired. Must be all the baby talk."

I collapse next to her, one hand on her thigh. "Yeah, me too. I'm knackered. Drunk way too much vodka. I've definitely got a wonderful hangover waiting for me tomorrow. Looking forward to it. Bring it on I say."

Aimee turns to me, smiling. "No more hangovers for me. I bet you're jealous."

"Jealous? Of you sitting around all day, fantasising about sipping a glass of Prosecco? I don't think so, Aim. But don't worry—I'll be happy to keep you occupied."

"Oh, and how do you plan to do that?"

"You can pick me and the guys up when we've been drinking. We'll save a fortune on taxis. I mean, we've got a little one on the way. We've got to watch the pennies."

"No way, boy. You can still get taxis. I'm not going to be your personal chauffeur. I'll be too busy relaxing, watching *Downton Abbey*, keeping our baby safe and sound in our house. No gallivanting around in the car with a bunch of drunken idiots." She rubs her stomach and redirects her voice to our unborn child. "Isn't it, Lucy. Mummy's gotta stay home and watch daytime TV. Hasn't she?"

"Lucy? Since when is she called Lucy? I told you I hate that name. I thought we agreed on Isobel if it's a girl, and Iron Man if it's a boy."

"*See?* That's exactly why men shouldn't get a say on the name. They just don't have a clue."

"Isobel is much nicer. Lucy's too common. We don't want our baby to be common, do we? I mean, she's already half-common with you as a mother."

Aimee chuckles, shaking her head. "Right, now

there's absolutely *no chance* of sex tonight."

My face lights up. "I take it back. You're not common and I can get Nia to drive us 'round instead. I'm sure she won't mind."

Aimee gets up from the couch. "Come on then, let's get this over with. I've got work tomorrow."

I get up as well. "*Charming.* You really know all the right things to say."

As we walk up the stairs, something suddenly occurs to me. "Are we allowed to have sex?"

"Of course we are. Why?"

"Well, what if my dick pokes the baby in the face?"

Aimee rolls her eyes as we reach the landing. "You're just not that big, Matt."

"Cheeky bitch," I say, as I follow her into the bedroom.

Twenty-One

"Push, Aimee!" the midwife says, firmly. "Come on, you can do it! You're nearly there! Just a little further!"

My eyes can barely believe what I'm witnessing. I said I wouldn't look, that I'd stay at the top of the bed. But how can I resist the temptation, the urge. I have to look. See for myself. After all, this could be my only chance to see a baby being born.

My baby.

I see the head.

Holy fuck!

I see a face.

"Come on, Aimee," I say; half-excited, half-petrified. "It's almost out. *Come on. Come on. You can do it!*"

My attention is split between seeing my baby slowly coming into life, one millimetre at a time, and watching the torment and strain on Aimee's face; like a scene from a horror film.

Time starts to slow. The midwife's words are

buried in screams. I still have Aimee's hand. Her grip tightens.

It's almost out.

It's nearly here.

It's…

The midwife takes our howling baby girl and places her onto Aimee's chest. Aimee looks at our baby with tears streaming down her cheeks. She lets go of my hand to hold her. I kiss Aimee on her sweat-soaked forehead. She smiles at me.

I can barely remember cutting the cord. I know I did. I specifically requested it. But everything's a blur, like a cluttered dream. When I take our baby from Aimee, I cradle her, staring down into my daughter's beautiful blue eyes with an overwhelming sense of joy, mixed in with incredible relief. I have to sit down on the chair, still with her in my arms. Too scared that I might faint, that I might drop her. I've never fainted before, so today wouldn't be the best day to start.

My baby has stopped crying, her eyes are half-closed, her chubby cheeks bright red, her tiny head covered in wispy blonde hair. I fight hard not to cry.

I said that I wouldn't. Just couldn't understand why any man would. Only women cry.

But now here I am, a grown man, sobbing my heart out in front of my daughter.

Our little angel from Heaven.

A gift.

Isobel.

TWENTY-TWO

"Can I get you another coffee, Shirl?" Aimee asks Mum as she sets Isobel down in her Moses basket. Isobel's eyes are opening and closing, still drowsy from her last feed.

"No thank you, Aimee," Mum replies, waving her hand in protest. "I'll be off soon."

Aimee sits down on the armchair, just as Mum gets off the couch and walks over to the basket, leaving me slouched across the cushions, completely shattered—yet another sleepless night of crying and 4:00 a.m. feeds. I could easily just fall asleep right here, right now, just by closing my stinging eyes. Aimee says I should sleep in the spare room; she tells me that she's the one on maternity leave, so why should we both suffer. But I won't. I hate sleeping away from them. Maybe it's just the loneliness of being in a single bed again; memories of living back home with Mum. Or it could be the simple fact that I miss them every moment that I'm away. Never thought I'd feel like this...so fatherly.

But here I am, ready to pass out on the couch, a combination of fatigue, stress, and work.

God knows how people cope with twins.

Mum leans over Isobel and sniffs her forehead. "I can't get enough of that smell. Reminds me of you, Matt—when you were this age. You never forget that smell. I tell you, if they could bottle it, they'd make a bloody killing."

"Tell you what, Mum," I say, eyes-half closed, "why don't you take one of her nappies home and sniff that. I'm sure that smell will take you back a few years."

Mum rolls her eyes at me. "No, it's all right, Matt. I'll stick with the forehead if it's all the same to you."

Mum kisses Isobel on the top of her soft head, and then glances around the living room. "You two have done a marvellous job in this house. You really have. Didn't notice the colour when I walked in. What is that?"

"It's called 'Almost Oyster'," Aimee replies, fulfilment in her tone as she also inspects the walls. "We got it on sale. Painted most of the house with it. Much better than that boring magnolia."

"Oh, yes," Mum agrees, "*Much* better. It really goes with the light-brown carpet. I like it a lot."

"What are you both talking about?" I interrupt, suddenly feeling a little more awake. "It looks exactly the same. It's just cream. There's no difference. You're both mad. And blind."

Aimee and Mum shake their heads in unison. "*Men*," Mum says.

"*Yep*," Aimee continues. "They just don't have a clue, do they Shirl? All they're interested in is cars and big TVs."

I sit up on the couch, now fully awake. "Well, for one, you know as well as I do that I have *no* interest in cars. And secondly—do you *see* a big TV?"

Mum looks over at the fifty-inch plasma on top of the glass cabinet. "Looks pretty big to me," she says, a confused frown on her brow. "What's wrong with it?"

"*Exactly*," Aimee says. "There's nothing wrong with it? It's big enough."

"You women just don't understand. I wanted a

projector on the wall. Big speakers. The works. But no—I had to stick with our old *calculator*-sized screen instead."

"It's not that bad," Aimee says. "It's fine for now."

Mum grabs her cream-coloured winter coat from the arm of the sofa chair. "You can't have big speakers with this little one anyway. You could damage her eardrums. They're very delicate at her age."

"Well, that's why I told him that he'd have to wait," Aimee points out, smugly, "until Isobel was older."

"*Yeah, yeah*," I say, as I get up to see Mum out. "Whatever. You'll just have to miss out on watching *Downton Abbey* on a hundred-inch screen, won't you. You can watch it in the bedroom on that minuscule thirty-incher. See how you cope with that."

Mum buttons up her coat and walks over to Isobel, peering down with adoring eyes. "Well, I best get a move on. I've had a lovely afternoon."

"There's no need to rush off so soon, Shirl," Aimee says. "Why don't you stay for dinner? You're more than welcome to join us."

"No, no, I've got to be off," Mum replies. "Don't like driving too late in the afternoon." She leans down and kisses Isobel on the forehead again. "See you later, sweetheart."

Even though I'm exhausted, a smile still creeps across my lips. It's so great to see Mum happy again. I think she's finally okay with living without me. *It's only taken her about two bloody years.*

"Right then," Mum says, "that's me done." She kisses me on the cheek, and then Aimee. "I'll see you all really soon."

We follow Mum to the front door.

"See you on Halloween," Aimee says. "You sure it's okay for you to watch the baby?"

"Of course it is," Mum replies. "I'm looking forward to it. You kids have a good time."

I open the front door; Mum steps out onto the pavement. "Thanks, Mum," I say. "See you in few days. Love you."

She blows a kiss as she walks up to her car. "Love you both. Give her a big kiss from me later."

She climbs into her car, gives us a wave, and

then drives off down the street. Aimee and I both look at each other, and then groan simultaneously in relief.

"Thank God for that," Aimee says.

"It wasn't *that* bad," I say, closing the front door. "Thought she'd be *much* worse."

Aimee grins. "I know. I'm only teasing you. She's fine. I enjoyed today. She's been a real help with everything."

We return to the living room and sit back down on the couch. "I'm so tired," I say, yawning, hands clasped together, arms outstretched above. "What time is it?"

Aimee checks her watch. "2:45 p.m."

"Is that all it is?"

Aimee nods.

"Really?"

She parades the time right up to my face. "Look for yourself if you don't believe me."

"I believe you, Aim. I'm just shocked how bushed I am—and it's still so early."

"Well, you're just getting old, Matt. Tiredness is the first sign."

"I thought it was grey hair."

Aimee leans in close to my head, examines my hair with her fingers. "You've definitely got a few greys coming through."

Laughing, I move my head away from her hand. "Get lost, butt-face."

* * *

Only six-thirty and it's already dark. How depressing. God knows how I'm gonna cope when the clocks go back. Or is it forward? I can never remember. All I know is that I hate the long, cold nights. So roll on summer!

Aimee is upstairs, bathing Isobel. I should help her really, but I'm way too shattered. Slumped on the couch, wearing just my old *Oasis* concert T-shirt and my *Simpsons* pyjama-bottoms, I check the planner on the TV, searching for a film Aimee recorded for me last week. Some crappy '80s horror, *The Stuff*. Something about a yogurt that kills people, or possesses people. One of the two…or maybe both. Can't really remember now. Easy watching because my brain has lost all its basic functions since the baby's arrived. I can't remember where I put things, people's names, appointments. I can't follow movie plots, TV programmes. Nothing. They say it's only the mother that gets baby-brain—but now I have my doubts.

I find the movie and play it, not really in the mood to watch it, but happy for the distraction. After perhaps twenty-minutes of terrible dialogue and atrocious acting, I hear Aimee calling from the landing. I get up off the couch like a fat pig and walk over to the staircase. "What's wrong?" I shout up to her. "Everything all right?"

"Can you come up and take her."

"Okay," I reply, as I make my way up the stairs with tired, heavy legs like iron.

Aimee is sitting on the edge of our bed, Isobel cradled in her arms. I smile when I see how my little angel's face looks, wrapped tightly in a pink towel, her hair and face still damp from the bath water.

"Can you dry her and put a fresh nappy on? I'm going to jump in the bath and have a soak. Do you mind?"

"Of course I don't mind," I reply, joining her on the bed.

She carefully hands her over to me, and I can't resist kissing her soft forehead.

"I won't be long," Aimee says, removing her white dressing gown and heading for the bathroom. With just her blue underwear on, Aimee still looks as stunning as ever. Yeah, she may have put on a few pounds since having Isobel, but none of that bothers me. All I see is a perfect wife, willing to sacrifice anything for our baby. And that's all that matters to me.

"Did you have a nice bath?" I say to Isobel in a childlike voice, as I lay her at the centre of the double bed, unravelling the towel. "Did you have fun with Mammy? Did you splash her?" My heart melts when I see that gorgeous grin spread across her rosy cheeks. *It's probably wind, but who the hell cares?*

Drying her from head to toe, I can't help but feel paranoid that she might be cold. I reach over to the radiator; it's warm. *Shit. Maybe she's too warm.*

I take a clean nappy from the top drawer of the oak chest, and put it on her.

When is she going to start talking? Can't wait to hear those precious first words. It's strange…I really want to savour every waking moment, but I still can't wait for her to grow up, to laugh, to tell me about her day, to sing, whistle, run, to bring me home a painting from school. All those things and a million more. I'll count the minutes until they arrive.

But a teenage Isobel?

Hell no!

Couldn't think of a worse fate for a father. All those horny bastards sleazing over *my* little girl. Feeding her bullshit lines just to get her into bed.

Well not on my watch!

I lean down and kiss Isobel on the cheek. "They'll never mess you around, will they? Daddy won't let them, will he?"

Let's just hope she doesn't end up resenting me, and marrying a serial killer just to get back at me.

Grabbing a clean vest and pyjamas from the drawer, I bring them over to the bed. Placing my palm behind her delicate head, I start to lift it gently, pulling her vest over it. I hate dressing her. I'm always worried that I'm hurting her. It doesn't seem to bother Aimee though. They were born to do this shit. They were born to be mothers. For me, it takes a little longer. Even though sometimes I—

The sound of wild splashing travels towards me.

"Aimee?" I call out to her. "You all right in there?"

No reply.

I hear splashing again.

"Aimee?" I repeat, making my way over to the bathroom. I push the door open and peer inside. "Is everything—"

I gasp in horror.

Aimee is thrashing around the bathtub, her head completely submerged under the water.

Adrenalin surging, I reach into the water, grab hold of her left arm and try to pull her out.

But I can't.

Her body is stuck to the bottom.

The water's too deep to pull her head out, so I secure both her wrists and pull as hard as I can.

She still won't budge.

I try again. But it's no use.

Her body squirming, soapy-water splashing

243

everywhere, I quickly yank the plug out, and then pick up the plastic jug from the floor. I start to scoop out the water as fast as humanly possible, throwing the contents over the tiles.

One. Two. Three jugs.

Then I lose count.

Once the water line is close enough, I drop the jug into the bath, and then grab Aimee's head, pulling it up to the surface.

Fuck! It's still an inch away from the top.

I pick up the jug again and start to scoop out more water. She's barely moving, prompting me to scoop even faster.

And faster.

Almost there.

Faster.

Half an inch.

My pulse is racing.

Just one more jug-full.

Just one...

Aimee bursts out of the water; eyes bloodshot, filled with terror. I yank her body half out of the bathtub as she coughs up water, struggling to breathe.

"*Jesus Fucking Christ, Aim,*" I blurt out, my body trembling, still in shock.

She tries to speak between coughs but she can't.

But then clarity hits me like a bus—and I work out exactly what Aimee is trying to say.

ISOBEL!

I storm out of the bathroom, almost slipping in the pools of water on the floor.

In a split second I'm back in our bedroom.

My chest tightens.

The bed is empty.

I can't breathe. I hurry to the other side of the bed to see if she's rolled off. The carpet is empty. Impossible!

Where the fuck is she?

Dropping to my knees, I check under the bed. It's bare, apart from a few stray shoes.

Please God let me find her!

Don't do this to me!

"Where is she, Matt?" Aimee asks from the bedroom doorway; her tone filled with alarm; her naked body dripping water over the floor.

I have no answer.

"Where the hell is she?" she repeats; this time a lot firmer.

I stand up, eyes scanning the floor and room, hoping that somehow I've missed her. "*She was right here,*" I stutter "*On the centre of the mattress.*"

Aimee pulls the quilt off the bed, then the pillows. "Then where the *fuck* is she, Matt?" she asks; her voice quivery; her hands shaking. "*She's not here.*"

I don't reply. There's nothing to do but look for her now. Nothing else matters.

I open the wardrobe doors and separate the hanging clothes. She's not there, just more shoes and other junk.

"Stop!" Aimee shouts. "We need to listen for her."

I stand completely still like a sculpture, trying to listen out for Isobel. Maybe the sound of her breathing. Crying. Any signs of movement.

Every second of silence feels like a lifetime. An eternity. A death sentence. Where the fuck is she? How could she be missing? It doesn't make sense.

It's just not possible.

She was right there…on the bed.

Safe.

Happy.

This is not happening…

Just as I'm about to leave the bedroom, to ransack the rest of the house, to check that the front door is locked, I hear something.

The faint sound of movement.

Breathing.

"Do you hear that?" I ask Aimee.

Aimee shakes her head; tear-filled eyes wide open.

Creeping across the room, breath held, body hunched, I try to follow the sound.

It's coming from the chest of drawers.

Stomach somersaulting, I grasp the two handles and slide open the top drawer.

Nothing. Just clean nappies, wet-wipes, and other baby things.

Then the second.

Nothing again. Just Aimee's underwear.

Body trembling, I open the third and final

drawer.

Please God let it be her.

Please God.

Don't do this to me.

Please…

An irrepressible wash of tears comes over me when I see Isobel lying there, just a vest and nappy on, looking up at me. No weeping. No stress. Like nothing had happened. Like the world was just how she left it. Aimee is next to me, on her knees, sobbing loudly.

She delicately takes Isobel out of the drawer and cradles her, kissing the top of her head. Aimee then looks at me, with those eyes. The same eyes I saw the day Isobel was born.

Eyes of pure relief, happiness and horror, all rolled into one.

"Get dressed," I say, sharply. "We're leaving."

I take Isobel from Aimee and finish dressing her on the bed. Aimee races around the bedroom, throwing clothes on. To Hell with packing. There's nothing here of importance. Nothing worth staying for.

Dying for.

"Take the baby downstairs," Aimee orders me, "and put some milk and a few bottles in a bag. And get some money."

"All right," I reply, grabbing one of Aimee's discarded shopping bags from the side of the bed. I then pull out a handful of nappies and a pack of wipes from the drawer, and stuff them into the bag. "Be quick. We're out of this house in twenty seconds. Okay?"

"I know."

She waves her hand to rush me out, but I'm already leaving. I'm downstairs in a second, Isobel tight to my chest. I hurry into the kitchen and grab my jacket from the back of the chair. I slip it on and then pat the pockets down for my wallet. Feeling its weight in the left pocket, I grab the car keys from the hook by the backdoor. I reach into the cupboard and pull out a tub of baby-formula, two empty bottles, and then shove them into the bag. Scanning the kitchen, I look for anything else I can just grab to take with us, just in case. But there's nothing we need. I go into the living room and do the same. I see some cash on the coffee table and scoop it up. It's just a few pound, but it might come in handy.

Pacing the bottom of the stairs, Isobel starts to cry. She's hungry. *Jesus Christ! Not now.* There's no time to make up a bottle. We have to leave right now!

"Come on, Aimee!" I yell up to her, my body tightening as Isobel's sobbing increases. "We have to go! Isobel needs milk!"

I hear the sound of feet stomping upstairs. "Coming!" Aimee shouts down, and then I see her at the top of the staircase, holding a red overnight bag.

"You got everything?" I ask her, urgency in my voice.

Aimee opens the bag, takes a quick peek inside, and then nods. "Yeah. Let's go."

But before Aimee's foot even touches the top step, she loses her balance, and plummets forward. Eyes wide with horror, Aimee scrambles to grab the banister but misses, slamming her chest against it instead. With Isobel still in my grasp, I'm powerless to help her as she starts to roll violently, cracking her head hard against the wall. The sound of wild drums echoes towards me as she bounces off each step. Within seconds, she's at the bottom of the stairs; face down on the carpet.

Horrified, I lay Isobel on the floor and race to Aimee. I turn her unconscious body over, and I'm nearly sick when I see the blood, dripping profusely from a gash at the left side of her head.

"*Aimee*," I say to her, as I gently shake her shoulders. "*Wake up. Please!*"

She doesn't respond—and now the baby's cries have become deafening. "*Please, Aimee. Say something.*"

I feel for a pulse on her neck.

I find one.

Is she breathing? *Please let her be breathing!*

Just as I bring my ear to her mouth to listen, something catches the corner of my eye.

Someone is standing at the top of the stairs.

A teenage girl.

I struggle to breathe as I stare into the girl's eyes.

Those dark, cold…*lifeless eyes.*

I know those eyes.

I know that grey dress, that black hair.

Somehow I no longer hear Isobel's cries. Somehow I no longer fear for Aimee's life. My eyes are too fixated on this girl, standing at the top of the stairs. Nothing else seems to matter. And my eyes remain locked until I watch her fade into oblivion. Like the memory of a dream, or the face of a stranger.

But this girl is no stranger.

I know this girl.

It's Lucy.

Her name is Lucy John.

TWENTY-THREE

It's just gone midnight and Aimee has started to stir.

For the past two hours I've been sitting next to her hospital bed, completely drained of life, waiting for her eyes to open. No one really knows why it's taking so long for her to wake. The doctor says it's probably just the concussion. But I know it's the stress of almost drowning and losing Isobel. I didn't tell the doctor what happened. How could I? What the hell would I even say? They'll laugh in my face; strap a straitjacket on me. And who the hell would blame them!

But it happened. Right in front of me.

I saw it with my own two eyes.

Aimee was held down under that water. Drowning. She wasn't sleeping. She wasn't hallucinating.

And she was pushed down those stairs. It wasn't an accident. It wasn't a coincidence. And it wasn't a freak of nature.

It was *Her*.

All *Her...*

"Aimee," I whisper, as I watch her slowly come to, her eyes straining to open. "Can you hear me? It's Matt."

She painfully winces when she turns her head, exploring the room, clearly disoriented.

"You're in the hospital, Aim. You're safe."

And then her eyes widen as if horrified, causing me to clench up in fright.

"*Isobel?*" she croakily blurts out, springing up into an upright position; IV stand nearly toppling over. She then recoils in pain, grasping her bandaged ribs.

I leap off my chair and place my hands on her shoulders, trying to settle her. "She's fine," I reassure her. "She's safe. Your parents have her. They left with her a few hours ago."

Breathing heavily, clearly still in a state of shock, she grabs my forearm roughly, and then pulls me close. "*I didn't fall down the stairs.*" Her fingernails start to dig deep into my skin, through my sweatshirt. "*Someone pushed me!*"

Prising her grip from my arm, I try to calm her down. I take her hand and stare into her eyes. "I

254

know, Aimee. It's all right. I believe you."

"You saw something. *Didn't you?*"

I nod, trying to disguise the guilt I feel, surging through my body.

"What did you see?" she asks, twisting the top of the blanket with both hands.

"I saw someone at the top of the stairs. Right after you fell."

"Who did you see?"

"I saw a girl."

"Who was it?"

Should I lie? Tell her that I have no idea?

No—I'm tired of this bullshit!

No more lies!

No more secrets!

I brace myself, take a breath, and then say, "Her name is Lucy John."

"Who the hell is Lucy John?" she asks, grimacing hard, covering her broken ribs again, as if the stress is worsening the pain.

I pause before answering. Can't face telling her. I'd give anything to walk out that door, just to avoid this conversation. But I can't. It's too late. I have to tell her the truth. I can't run from it anymore. I can't bury it any deeper.

"Lucy was my girlfriend," I tell her—my words brimming with disgrace. "She died twenty years ago."

Aimee's face drops when she hears the words. I've never seen her with such a look on her face. So lost; confused. *So disturbed.* "And she was in *our house?*" Aimee says. "In *our flat? All this time?*"

I nod, struggling to meet her eyes.

"But you've never mentioned her before, Matt," she points out. "Why did you keep it from me?"

I pull the chair away from the side of the bed, and twist it around so that it's facing Aimee. And then I sit. "I don't know. I think I repressed it all. Pushed her away. Well, at least I thought I did."

"How long have you known?"

"Only tonight. When you fell."

"Jesus, Matt, I can't believe you would keep something like that from me? After everything we've been through."

"I know, Aim. I'm sorry. I just didn't think you needed to know. It was such a long time ago."

"I've told you about every ex-boyfriend that I've ever had. Any ordinary person would think to mention an ex that *died*. So why did you keep it from me? What aren't you telling me, Matt? Come on— *spit it out.*"

I don't answer. It's too hard. But I have to. There's no avoiding this now.

"Come on, Matt," she says, her tone laced with displeasure, "tell me the truth. What happened to her? Did you *hurt her?*"

I don't respond again. But then I catch a glimpse of her eyes. And suddenly I see them transform from a look of disturbance…to disgust.

"Did you kill her?" she asks, in a half-joking tone, as if battling with the possibility that I might actually be capable of something so vile.

"It's not that simple, Aim."

"What's not that simple? It's a simple question, Matt. There's only one answer. Did you kill this girl—*yes or no?*"

Suddenly I can see my life with Aimee flashing before my eyes. From our first date, to our wedding day. Everything in high definition. From the smell of flowers I got for her the week after we met, to the churning feeling of excitement and fear when we brought Isobel home from the hospital.

"*No*," I say, with pure conviction, eyes locked firmly on hers. "I didn't kill her."

"Then what the hell happened, Matt? I wanna know *everything*. No more secrets. Just the truth."

"All right," I say, with a crippling knot in my stomach. "I'll tell you everything."

TWENTY-FOUR

There's a teenage girl with long black hair sitting on the swing. She's gorgeous and she's staring at me. What the hell is she doing in a dump like this? Should I talk to her? Tell her that I like her?

No, too forward. She'll tell me to fuck off.

Oh shit! She's coming over!

I swallow a mouthful of vodka, wipe my lips and chin, and pray to God that I don't have food in my teeth.

"You gonna share that, or what?" she asks as she sits next to me on the bench, so close I can feel her hip touching mine.

I shake my head, handing her the bottle. I don't smile though; I play it cool instead.

She swigs the vodka and then passes it back to me. "Thanks."

"It's no problem," I say, as if pretty girls sit next to me all the time. "So where are your friends? I thought girls were afraid of the dark."

"I could say the same about you," she replies,

smiling with perfect teeth.

"I don't see much of my friends these days," I reply, and then take a giant gulp of vodka.

She snatches the bottle and takes another swig. "Is that why you're drinking?"

I shake my head.

She swivels on the bench with her blue eyes glowing with intrigue. "So come on then—what's your story?"

"I don't have a story," I reply, shaking my head. "I'm just drinking."

She chuckles. "That's bullshit. Teenage boys drink with friends at parties. Troubled teens drink alone at night in parks." She nudges me softly. "So come on, spit it out. You can trust me."

I haven't told anyone about Dad. Why would I tell a complete stranger?

Because she's gorgeous, that's why.

She gives me the bottle, and then tuts loudly. "Suit yourself. Have fun drinking alone, *loser.*"

She gets up off the bench and starts to walk towards the playground exit.

I don't want her to leave.

"*Fine*," I call out. "I'll tell you."

The girl stops in her tracks, turns to me and beams with obvious satisfaction. "Good choice."

"It's my father," I say as she sits back down. "He's been cheating on my mother."

"Oh, right. That's tough. Are they going to split up?"

"No. *Well*, not yet anyway. I'm the only one who knows. I caught them *fucking* in my parents' bed. Some whore from his office."

"Dirty bastard!" She takes a swig of vodka. "Do you think you'll end up telling your mother?"

"No. I couldn't do that to her. Or him. He begged me not to tell Mum, and he swears blind that he still loves her, that it was a one off."

"Do you believe him?"

I shrug. "I want to."

The girl puts her hand over mine as it rests on my thigh. It sends a strange tingle up my arm and around my body. It feels good, but I don't show it.

"Just keep an eye on him," she says. "Make sure he keeps his promise."

"Yeah, I will."

She slides her fingers between mine and squeezes my hand gently. I can't quite believe how forward she's being. *Is this a prank?*

"So what's your story then?" I ask.

"Where do I start?" She takes another gulp of vodka. "Well, my Dad left us when I was ten. Fucked off to Australia with some slut from Bristol. My bitch of a mother is a raging alcoholic who thinks that it's my fault the old prick left." She takes another swig, this time finishing the bottle, and then launching it into the bushes behind us. "*Oh*, and my brother, the only one in my screwed up family that I actually cared about, decided to tie a rope around his neck three weeks ago and hang himself in our shed. So other than that—life's pretty uneventful."

Jesus Christ. I'm lost for words, almost gasping in shock. All of sudden my problems seem a lot less significant.

She looks to me, with completely dry eyes, and somehow throws me another smile. "I'm Lucy by the way?"

I try to return a smile but I can't; my lips are frozen from amazement.

"I'm…Matt," I stutter.

She pulls her hand out of mine and runs her fingers through my hair, pulling my head towards hers. "Nice to meet you, Matt," she says, just before our lips meet.

Holy fucking shit! This has got to be the weirdest night of my life.

After maybe a minute, Lucy pulls her mouth away from mine, and then takes my hand again. "We need more booze," she announces with eagerness "There's a shop up the road?

"I'm out of money though."

"Yeah, me too," Lucy says as she yanks me up off the bench.

"Then where are we going?"

"To get booze," she replies, steering me towards the playground exit. "We're just not gonna pay for it."

* * *

I painfully swallow the chalky pill. I'm okay with painkillers, vitamins, but there's something about

263

ecstasy that always makes me retch. Lucy laughs as I struggle to hold back the bile that's desperate to leave my stomach. I grab my can of beer, take a huge gulp, and the urge to puke quickly disappears.

"You're a lightweight, babe," she says as she drops her pill onto her tongue, and then swallows it without flinching.

Grabbing her thin waist, I pull her backwards on my bed until her head is on the pillow. I grasp her hips and move her body closer, kissing her on the lips at the same time.

"I love you, Matt," Lucy whispers.

"I love you too," I reply, my hand on her arse, pulling her even closer.

Suddenly the door bursts open, causing our bodies to swiftly part.

It's Dad.

"The school just called, Matt," he says with a pissed off tone. "They said you've been suspended for fighting."

"So what?" I retort, shrugging. "The boy tried stealing my phone. What the fuck was I meant to do?"

"Watch you're language, boy!"

Lucy gets up off the bed, squaring up to him. "Why don't you just get off his back?"

Dad snorts. "Excuse me?"

"You're the reason he's fighting," Lucy continues. "You fucked up his life."

"Who the hell do you think you're speaking to?" Dad asks, his eyes wide with rage. "This is *my* bloody house. So you're lucky I don't throw you out."

"Leave it, Luce," I say, taking hold of her hand. "It's not worth it."

Lucy pulls out of my grip and points her finger at Dad's chest. "You need to cut Matt some slack," she barks at him, "unless you want us to have a little *chat* with Shirl. Tell her all about the little *mistress* you've been fucking."

The colour drains from Dad's cheeks. "You don't know what you're talking about?"

"Yes I do," she replies. "Matt and I tell each other everything. We don't keep secrets." Lucy chortles. "I can't say the same about you."

Dad tries to retort but no words leave his

mouth. All he can do is shake his head and back away like a frightened weasel.

Lucy nods her head with a look of accomplishment.

"You promised you wouldn't tell your mother," Dad squirms. "It'll break her."

"Don't pretend you're doing this for her," I say with a tone of disgust. "This is all for you."

Dad steps out onto the landing. "Just don't tell her. *Please, Matt.*"

"Then stay the fuck out of Matt's business," Lucy snaps, "and maybe we'll do the same."

She closes the door practically in his face.

I almost feel sorry him. But then I think about the day I caught him with that *slag*, and all my sympathy goes up in smoke.

Lucy climbs back onto the bed and rests her head on the pillow. She grabs my hips and pulls me towards her. "Where were we?"

* * *

"What the hell have you done?" I tell Lucy as I

frantically wrap the towel around her bleeding forearm. "You've gone too deep this time. You could've been killed."

"It's fine," she calmly replies, as if it's nothing more than a paper cut. "You sound like my bitch of a mother."

The blood has already started to soak through the towel, so I press down hard to stop the bleeding. "She probably didn't mean to throw his things out. Maybe they got mixed up with the rubbish."

Lucy shakes her head with a cold smirk. "No. That bitch knew *exactly* what she was doing. She's glad my brother's dead. One less person to worry about."

Moving the sweat-soaked hair from her bloodshot eyes, I can see that she's been crying. She'd never admit it though. "So what are you going to do now?" I ask.

Next to the knife on my bedside cabinet there's a can of beer. She picks it up, opens it, and then downs it in one. "Well I'm not going back there. And if she tries to find me then she'll have another black eye."

"You can stay here with me," I say with enthusiasm. "I'm sure Mum won't mind."

Lucy snorts. "What—here? With your wanker of a dad?"

"Well what's the alternative? Sleeping on the streets?"

She falls silent for moment as if mulling over her options. "I suppose I could crash here." She kisses me on the lips. "As long as I'm with you—that's all that matters."

"I'll ask Mum when she gets home. Pointless asking Dad; he's too much of a coward to say no."

Lucy smiles and then kisses me again. "You're all I have left in the world. I don't know what I'd do if I lost you."

"You're not going to lose me."

* * *

"You lied to me!" I scream at Dad. "You said it was just a one-off!"

"They're just texts, Matt," Dad says as he tries to snatch his mobile phone from my hand. "I'm not having an affair with her. *Honestly.*"

I move the phone out of reach. "You're full of shit!" I yell, backing away into the kitchen. "I'm not stupid!"

"Please, Matt," Dad says, almost in tears. *"I'm begging you. Don't do this."*

I shake my head. "It's too late! I fucking warned you!"

The sound of a car pulling up onto the drive fills the room.

Mum's home.

* * *

"You're lying," I say, shaking my head. "Why would you say something like that?"

Mum gets up from the couch, eyes streaming, and walks over to me. "It's true, Matt," she says, taking both my hands. *"He's gone."*

"No," I say, pulling out of Mum's grasp. "He's just with that woman. That's all. He's not dead. *You're a liar!"*

I start to back away towards the front door,

refusing to let her lies seep in.

"I'm not, Matt," she replies as she follows me. "They found him by the train tracks."

"No!" I snap, my back against the door, my hand gripping the handle, ready to bolt down the street. "Dad wouldn't do that to us! He wouldn't leave us like that!"

She opens out her arms, inviting me in for a hug. *"Come here, Matt."*

Shaking my head in disbelief, my vision fogs over, and the walls start to move, pressing towards me.

Mum mouths something else, but I can't hear her words.

I can't hear anything.

The acid in my stomach erupts and I puke up over the floor. I wipe my mouth and then drop to my knees in tears. Mum kneels down beside me, her arm across my back, crying hard into my shoulder.

I can't catch my breath.

I need to get out of here.

I need to see him.

I need to see for myself—because this is all my fault.

And if it's true, if he is dead...then I really have lost everything.

* * *

The six-pack of beer doesn't touch the sides. Lucy is sitting next to me on the park bench, sobbing, begging me not to do this. To stay with her.

"I love you, Lucy," I tell her, my eyes dripping with tears, "but I can't deal with the guilt. It's too much."

Lucy puts her cold hands over my cheeks and pulls my head close to hers. "It's not your fault, babe. Your father was the one who made his choice. You were only looking out for Shirl. You had to tell her."

I don't respond; my mind racing, my vision clouding over, Mum's anguish just a distant problem. All I see is an image of Dad, dressed in his grey suit, standing on the train tracks—*waiting to die*.

I feel sick.

"*I won't let you go through with this,*" Lucy sobs. "*Not without me.*"

Her words somehow break through the fog, a glimmer of clarity returning. "What's that supposed to mean?"

"You know what it means. There's nothing left for me here. No brother, no friends, no parents. It's just you. It's *always* been you. And if I'm gonna die, then I want it to be next to you, not on the floor of some crack-den, or lying in a ditch at the side of the road. It has to be by your side. *Always*."

I start to cry—harder than ever before. Lucy wraps her arms around me and hugs me.

"*I don't want to die alone,*" I sob, my words muffled, barely audible.

"You don't have to," she replies, kissing the side of my neck. "*I'll never leave your side.*"

* * *

I take Lucy's hand as we head across the damp field. Everything seems dreamlike, surreal, like I've just dropped acid. My stomach is full of butterflies, but it's not from nerves or second thoughts. It's excitement. Excitement that all this pain, this suffering will be over soon—and Lucy will be with me all the way.

Forever.

"Ready?" she calmly whispers as we reach the train tracks.

I nod, squeezing her hand even tighter.

There's a rumbling sound in the distance.

The train is coming.

Stepping onto the tracks, I feel the floor beneath my feet vibrate.

I see Mum. She's standing over a grave. It belongs to me. It's right next to Dad's.

The roar of the train is deafening, rippling through my entire body.

Mum drops to her knees in grief, pounding her fist against the soft dirt, screaming for me to come back to her.

Lucy smiles at me, and tells me that she loves me. But I can't hear her, only read her lips.

I scream it back to her.

The sound of the horn bellows just metres from us.

We close our eyes and wait for everything to be over. To begin again. To reset.

I see Mum again. She's standing next to Dad, about to take a photo of me at the zoo.

I barely register my fingers slipping out of Lucy's hand.

Mum and I are sitting around a dinner table wearing blue and red paper hats. There's a huge smile on my face because it's Christmas day.

The train screams as it passes me, just inches from my feet; the heat and air hitting me hard in the face.

Something else hits my face as well. Something wet. Hands shaking, I touch my cheek.

It's Lucy's blood.

My scream gets lost in the roar of the train, taking a lifetime to disappear.

But I don't want it to stop. I want it to go on forever.

I don't want to see the tracks. I can't bear it.

Closing my eyes tightly, my body juddering in anguish, I lie back on the loose stones, and then I cry.

I'm sorry, Lucy.
Please forgive me.

I love you...

TWENTY-FIVE

"Aimee?" I say, softly, as if waking her. "Say something."

She doesn't respond.

"Please," I persist, "talk to me. Say something. *Anything.*"

Taking her hand away from her mouth, Aimee sniffs loudly, wiping her eyes and nose with her wrist. "What's there to say?" she asks, coldly. "You've said it all."

"Please, Aimee, don't be like that. It wasn't exactly the easiest thing to tell you. I've never told anyone about this. Just you."

"Lucy John knows."

"Lucy John is dead."

"She's not *dead*, Matt!" Aimee snaps. "She's very much alive! And she has been all this time! She's been watching us for years, getting angrier and angrier with every day that she can't be with you. Everything we've done, everything we've been through, moving in together, getting married, having

Isobel, all that, all those great things have just added more and more fuel to the fire. The fire that *you* started!"

"Look, you don't know how hard it was for me," I say. "*You* didn't have to sit next to Lucy's mother in the funeral, listening to her cry. She'd already lost her son to suicide, and now she had to bury her daughter too. That's what *I've* had to live with. That's what *I've* had to swallow every time I think about that night. And it never goes away. So tell me what I was supposed to do, Aimee? How the hell was I supposed to know what the repercussions would be? Tell you that there's a chance that my *dead-ex-girlfriend* might still be *pissed* with me?"

"Don't joke, Matt. None of this is funny. She tried to kill me."

"I'm not joking. I'm serious! What would you have done in my shoes?"

"*I would have told you the truth!*"

"I wanted to. So many times. But I just couldn't bring myself to do it. Everything's always gone so well for us. I just didn't want to rock the boat. It was easier *not* to tell you."

"It's *always* easier. But that still doesn't change the fact that you lied. You kept something so huge from me. From your own *wife*. The one person you *could* tell. I would *never* do that to you! *Ever!*"

"I'm sorry, Aimee," I plead. "I never meant for any of this to happen."

Aimee starts to cry again. "*She took our baby, Matt. She took our baby from us. She tried to drown me. I couldn't breathe. Do you have any idea what that's like? Do you? I can't live like this. I can't live in fear anymore. If she wants you...she can have you. Isobel and I won't be coming back to that house...until Lucy's gone. It's not safe... It never has been!*" Aimee sniffs, just about managing to control her anguish. "She's won, Matt. It's obvious that all this is about you. She doesn't really care about Isobel. Or me. All she wants is you! She wants to hurt you! And the only way to really do that is to hurt the people you love. So I won't be a part of it any longer."

"What if I can't get rid of her? What am I supposed to do then?"

"I don't know, Matt. I really don't. But you won't see us until you figure it out."

I almost tell her that she's wrong, that I can protect them—but that would be a stone-faced lie.

"We have to think about Isobel," she continues, "and that means leaving you behind. It's the only way. Moving house was never enough. She'll find us wherever we go. Your mother's house, my parents' house. China. Australia. Nowhere is safe. Not anymore."

"How am I supposed to fix this?" I ask, battling to hold back my anguish. "Confront her? Tell her to leave us alone? Call another medium? What? Tell me!"

"I don't know, Matt," she says, frostily. "But I don't want you here right now. I'm too afraid that she'll come back for me. For Isobel. So you need to go."

I'm lost for words. My brain can't quite register what's happening. I feel sick, lightheaded. Need to sit down, but I can't. I need to leave. I need to do what she says. Aimee's right. It's not safe to be around me. Lucy wants me—*she always has*. At least I finally know who I'm dealing with. Maybe I can talk to her. To make amends. Tell her that I'm sorry.

279

Tell her why I left her on the track. Maybe she'll leave us alone then. Maybe that's all she needs.

To be at peace.

My chin starts to quiver when I say goodbye to Aimee. She sobs when I kiss her on the lips, when I tell her that I love her, that I'll miss them both more than she could ever know.

I leave the room, not looking back. It's too hard. I just keep walking down the corridor, past the nurse station, and out into the reception, fighting with every grain of strength I have in my heart not to break down, to fall to my knees in turmoil. I have to stay strong. I have to find a solution. I should have told Aimee everything long ago. But I was stupid. A fucking *idiot*.

But no more bullshit.

No more running.

This ends tonight.

TWENTY-SIX

The cold night air hits me, biting at my cheeks as I step out of the car. I feel the odd speck of rain land on my neck, so I look up at the sky; it's black with grey clouds overhead. There's a storm coming.

I peer up at the house and have that same feeling of foreboding that I had when I looked up at the flat.

The lights are all still on in the house. Didn't even realise I left them on. The last thing that was on my mind was switching them off. But maybe I *did* knock them off. Maybe it was Lucy who put them back on. For all I know she's done it to show us that she's here for good, that this is her house now. Not mine. Not Aimee's. An animal marking its territory.

Locating the house key from the bunch, I point it at the lock, hand shaking nervously as I twist the key. The door opens and I gingerly enter the house. I fight hard to calm myself, to control the fear gushing around my body, but every step I take, every movement, every sound I hear, only amplifies this feeling of threat.

As soon as I'm in the living room, I start to scan every inch like a frightened child. My heart is pounding. I try to steady it but it only worsens when I see the stairs. Eyes climbing one step at a time, I'm petrified that I'll see Lucy again, standing at the top, glaring down at me, eyes brimming with hatred, with bitterness.

But I don't. She's not there.

Creeping through the living room, I head into the kitchen. When I see that it's deserted, my pulse rate reduces a little. But then once the idea of venturing upstairs pops into my head, it starts to charge again.

But I have to go up there. Can't put it off.

I can't run from this.

I know she's here somewhere.

She's toying with me, watching me suffer.

At the foot of the staircase, I look to the top again. Vile, shocking images of Aimee plummeting down fill my head. And then I imagine Aimee holding Isobel while she falls. It sends a cold tremor down my spine. I shake off the image, take in a deep breath, and then start to climb the stairs. Halfway up, I peep through the railings, onto the landing. Even though I need to see her, need to talk to her, the terror that's rushing through my body is telling me to turn back, to leave this house...*for good*. But I have to ignore it. I have to do this. No matter what—otherwise I'll lose my family.

At the top of the stairs, I inspect the landing. No sign of Lucy. Holding onto the banister, I listen out for any movement, any whispers. There's nothing. Not even the faintest of rustles. Skulking across the landing, I head into Isobel's future nursery. The door creaks open and I hit the light switch; my body clenched in apprehension. Inside the pink room I see heaps of boxes still littered across the brown carpet, still unpacked from the move. So much junk, so many places for Lucy to hide. I step into the room and start to explore. I can't imagine Lucy being here, crouched behind a box. But what the hell do *I* know? I leave the room and head over to our bedroom. The door is slightly ajar. I anxiously prod it open with my fingers and step inside. The light is already on, which makes the ordeal marginally more bearable. Once the door is fully open, I can see the entire room. It's deserted. I exhale in relief and then leave the bedroom, heading towards the bathroom. At the doorway, I poke my head around the corner fretfully, half-expecting Lucy to be lying in the bathtub, or standing in the middle of the room. But she isn't. I'm torn between relief and disappointment. I want this to be over with, like tearing off a plaster, but the notion of being face to face with her, sends an icy, ominous chill over my skin. But the one time I actually *want* to see her, and she's not fucking here!

Heading back down the stairs, I think about Aimee and Isobel. What if I can't communicate with Lucy? What if it's impossible? What the hell am I supposed to do then? I can't exactly live here on my own. Live here with Lucy watching me, taunting me. Day after Day. Nights endless and hellish.

I'm in the living room and I feel nothing. No icy chill at the back of my neck. No ghostly moans. No chains rattling. No broken mirrors. No whispers of my name.

And no Lucy John.

Deflated, I sit on the couch, my throbbing, tired head resting back on the cushion, my eyes burning, longing for a few hours sleep. But I can't. I won't spend another night in fear, another night away from my family. She's here. Somewhere. I just know it.

Maybe five minutes of total silence passes and my eyes have finally shut. I keep seeing Isobel's beautiful face, her rosy cheeks, her baby-blue eyes. But then the image is replaced with Lucy dragging Isobel's helpless body off the bed, into the drawer, and slamming it shut. The vision causes my stomach to churn, so I try to think of something a little more positive. Our wedding maybe? Bringing Isobel home from the hospital? My first date with Aimee?

Just as my mind drifts off, dipping in and out of consciousness, something brings me back to the living room, back to reality. A sound. The sound of water running. My eyes spring open and I'm off the couch, muscles tensed, fists clenched, ready for war. I peer into the kitchen; the tap by the sink is still off. I follow the noise to the foot of the stairs. It's coming from the bathroom. I make my way up, each step causing my chest to tighten even more. At the top, I grasp the banister and edge around it towards the open bathroom door. I try to silence my heavy breathing, as if attempting to sneak up on a burglar. I creep just inches from the opening, petrified of what I might see in the bathtub.

You can do this, Matt!

I take a few deep breaths to prepare myself, and then leap into the bathroom.

The bathtub tap is running.

She's here.

Reaching over the tub, I grip the handle of the tap and start to twist. Suddenly I feel the room fill with an ice-cold breeze. I shudder as I straighten, checking the room again, convinced that she's here, waiting, watching me like she's always done. I glance up at the window just in case. It's closed. An awful sensation of dread creeps over my skin as I leave the bathroom, stepping out onto the landing. I still don't see her. But it's only a matter of time before I do. *I just know it. Feel it. She's toying with me.* I walk over to our bedroom. Just as my hand pushes the door open, I hear the sound of a glass smashing. It came from downstairs—in the living room. I follow the noise. Each step closer to the living room steals my breath, until by the last few steps, when the room is in full view, I can barely breathe.

I don't see Lucy.

Still tense, I examine the room to find the source of the noise. Nothing obvious leaps out at me; a smashed window perhaps; a vase; a wine glass. But then I see something glimmer on the floor next to the fireplace. A broken photo frame; tiny fragments of glass scattered across the carpet. I walk over to the fireplace and pick up the frame, shaking off the shards as I bring it up to see. It's a photograph of Aimee holding Isobel. It was taken just hours after she was born.

There are scratch marks over Isobel's eyes.

I feel sick, the image too much to bear. All of a sudden I feel weak, dizzy, my vision foggy, my legs like jelly. The walls and ceiling are closing in around me, pinning me, crushing me in a vice. Can't take anymore. Can't take this hell. Can't let her take my family.

I won't let her.

I won't let her win.

"WHAT THE FUCK DO YOU WANT, LUCY?" I shout, so loud that my voice echoes around the room. "TELL ME! I'M TIRED OF THESE GAMES!"

I listen for a response.

Nothing comes.

"WHAT DO YOU WANT ME TO DO?" I scream again. "TELL ME! I NEED TO KNOW! *PLEASE*!"

I'm so angry—*so terrified*—that I can't help but squeeze and twist the photo in my grip. I look down at it, straighten it out, but then drop it on the floor when I see the scratch marks again.

I listen hard for Lucy but still hear nothing. Just as I'm about to turn and search the house again, the living room quakes with a deafening bang. My heart violently jolts in fright. The TV, which was mounted to the wall, is now facedown on the floor, taking with it the metal bracket and a chunk of plaster. Body frozen, eyes wide, I slowly back away against the fireplace.

Another crashing sound!

This time from the kitchen. It's the sound of pots and pans being flung across the room, landing on the floor-tiles. I think about racing into the kitchen to see for myself, but I don't. Can't move. Can't prise my back away from the stone mantelpiece.

Then my attention goes to the staircase. Isobel's baby basket is tumbling down, rolling brutally as it hits each step, until it finally comes to a halt at the porch door.

Across the room, directly under the stairs, I can see the stereo moving heavily towards the edge of its shelf. And then it plummets towards the floor. The array of wires suspends it just inches from the floor, but then I hear a snapping noise and the stereo hits the carpet.

Something strikes the side of my face, cutting my cheek. It's a DVD case, flung from the shelf next to the TV. Then another hits me, this time I see it coming and I block it with my forearm. One of Aimee's glass ornaments flies towards me from the windowsill. It misses my head by an inch, smashing into a million pieces against the mantelpiece. I duck, avoiding the wedding photo frame hurtling across from the opposite wall. The mirror by the porch door shatters. The top glass panels of the kitchen door shatter. Then the bottom ones. The mirror behind me, above the mantelpiece explodes, splinters of glass raining over my hair and shoulders. Shaking the pieces off me like water, I move away, heading towards the porch door. *Can't stay here anymore. Gotta get the fuck out. Right now.* Reaching for the handle, I judder in fright as each panel of glass in the door bursts. I fly backwards, tripping up over the baby basket, and then hit the back of my head on the first step.

The room is spinning; my body glued to the floor; my eyelids desperate to close.

Am I asleep?

Is this a dream?

It has to be.

None of this is possible.

None of this...

There's an echo of something hitting the wall above me. Then another smashing sound from the other side of the room. My eyes spring open. A surge of clarity rushes through my body. I struggle to my feet, head pounding, legs weak and heavy. I look at the living room, at the mess; listen as objects are pitched through the air, breaking to pieces. The living room, the kitchen, the entire house is alive with noise, with movement, like a street riot.

Have to leave this house. It's not safe. There's no getting through to her. It's too dangerous.

I grasp the door handle and start to pull it open. The gap is mere centimetres before I feel something yank it out of my hands, slamming the door shut. I grab the handle again but it's welded shut. Using both hands, I pull as hard as I can, nearly passing out from the strain. But it's no use.

"WHAT THE FUCK DO YOU WANT FROM ME?" I bellow in desperation. "TELL ME!"

All of a sudden, the house falls dead silent.

I try to remain still, try to calm myself, maybe get through to her.

I wait.

And wait.

Still silence.

Where is she?

"*Iiiis…oooo…beeeeellll.*"

Once I feel the ice-cold whisper in my ear, I yank the handle and the porch door finally opens. My eyes in tunnel vision, I race towards the front door. I turn the lock and the door swings open; the cold winter rain hits my face instantly. I dart towards the car, soaking wet, not looking back, eyes fixed straight ahead. Pulling out my car keys from my pocket, I push the clicker and the door unlocks. I quickly clamber inside, start the engine, and speed off down the street. Away from the house.

Away from Lucy John.

Not really sure where the hell I'm heading to. Mum's? Ed's? A hotel maybe? Don't know where it's safe. Can't go to Aimee's parents' house. Can't risk it. And she'll never let me be that close to Isobel.

My cheek feels sore from the DVD case. I prod it gently, wincing in pain as my fingers touch damp skin. I'm bleeding. I glance up at the rear-view mirror to see the cut on my face.

"FUCK!"

Lucy is sitting in the backseat.

I swerve the car in fright, tyres slipping in the rain, hitting the curb hard. Straightening the steering wheel, the side of my head hits the window. Ignoring the shooting pain, I look at the back seat. It's empty, apart from Isobel's baby-seat. Clenching the steering wheel, knuckles white, I slam down the accelerator and race down towards the bypass.

Can't run from her.

Can't hide from her.

She's always with me.

Always watching.

Speeding down the long dark road, I pass a car. Then another. And another, nearly clipping an oncoming van. I keep accelerating. Not sure why. Not sure what I can achieve from it. She's already found me. I can't see any other cars for miles, just floods of rain pouring down from the sky, drowning the road like a river.

Just have to keep driving.

Without even realising, the speedometer has reached a hundred and thirty miles an hour. At the end of the bypass I see a roundabout. There are bushes to the left of it and houses to the right. I think about blasting straight on, powering through, regardless of any potential oncoming traffic. But instead I slam on the brakes and the car comes to an abrupt stop. Without a seatbelt on, my body jolts forward, cricking my neck as my head bounces back against the headrest. My foot slips off the clutch and the engine cuts out.

Breathing like I've just completed a marathon, the thought of opening the door and fleeing pops into my head. But my hands are fused to the steering wheel. Not from any power Lucy has over me. This time it's just an overwhelming feeling of loss and terror.

I start to sob in frustration, in futility. I try to fight it but the turmoil overpowers me.

Don't know what do to.

Need to end this nightmare.

End this hell.

Just wanna go home.

To my family…

Loud music suddenly bursts out of the car speakers.

Body jarring in shock, wincing as my eardrums throb, I rush to press the 'off' button and the music vanishes.

The deafening sound returns.

Once again I frantically switch it off.

"What do you want, Lucy?" I ask, bravely, ears ringing. "Tell me!"

I start to feel two cold hands slither down from the back of my neck, under my shirt, down to my chest. Just as I shake them off hysterically, I catch a glimpse of the rear-view mirror again.

Lucy is hovering behind my seat. I see her hands buried beneath my shirt; her eyes and smile wide; her skin pale and dull. I scream in horror, open the door, and then scramble out of the car. I fall onto the wet road, scraping both knees as I roll to a standing position. *And then I run.* Run as fast as I can in the torrential rain, over the grassy roundabout, then back onto the road towards the city. Don't think I've ever run so fast. I don't look back. Don't care if someone steals the car. *They can have it.* Need to keep moving. As far away from her as possible. Just have to keep—

"Where are you going, babe?" I hear Lucy whisper in my left ear.

Vision skewed, mind in tatters, I somehow pick the pace up even more.

I pray to find people, *any people.* Just someone to hide behind, to hold her off 'til morning. But as I sprint past the town hall, then past a school, and a row of shops, I realise that there's no one. Not for several hours. Not in this weather. I'm completely alone. No people. No cars. No buses. Not even police. It's just me and Lucy John.

By the time I reach the leisure centre, my heart and lungs are just about ready to explode. Can't breathe. Can't even see straight. Have to rest. Have to sit for a minute.

But I can't. Not now. Not here.

She's watching me.

Ignoring my willpower, I have to stop by the fire-station gates. Crouched over, hands on knees, I take in as much oxygen as I can. As the seconds pass, as my gasping for air decreases, I straighten. Glancing around the area, without the sound of my thrashing heart, my wheezing lungs, I notice how quiet the streets are. Not even a siren in the distance, or the sound of a delivery truck nearby. Just the rain, soaking my clothes through; freezing my ears, cheeks, and hands; blurring my view of everything. I start to walk down the street, body hunched from the cold, arms wrapped firmly around my chest. Not sure what the plan is, where I'm heading. Just walking. Just moving. Until the sun comes up. Until the city is once again alive with the sounds of cars and people.

My head is aching, trying to make sense of everything, battling hard to pluck out a solution. Can't run forever. Distance doesn't seem to be a problem for Lucy. In fact, it seems the more I run, the more it spurs her on. But what choice do I have? There's nothing I can do. There's nowhere safe for us to live. It's—

"There...you...are."

The words send an electric shock of terror through my body. Without even looking behind me I'm off again, sprinting down the street. I head towards the city centre again, doubling back.

I see Isobel's face in my head. And then Aimee's. She

297

cradling her, shushing her to sleep.

Why aren't I with them? Why aren't I there, holding her in my arms, rocking her gently to sleep?

Why the hell am I running in the middle of the night? In the middle of nowhere?

It's hopeless!

There's got to be a way out of this. Can't keep running. Have to keep my family safe. And they'll never be safe while Lucy is out there. She wants blood. *My* blood. She's pissed off with me. *Seething.* She wants to take away my family. Take away everything that matters to me. Just to hurt me. Just to be near me. To watch me. Can't live like this. It's been too long standing over my shoulder. Getting more bitter with every step forward I make. To a normal life. A normal family. Nothing like the life I left behind. Nothing like the life she lost. But I can't take back what I did to her. I wish I could, but I can't. I'd give anything to change it. Give anything to go back to that night. Go back to that moment in the park, or at the side of the tracks, and tell her that I was wrong about life, about pain. It can get better. Time really *is* the greatest of healers. It's not just a fantasy. There *is* hope out there. No matter how lost, how alone, how desperate you are, someone, somewhere, is out there for you; waiting to free you, to drag you from the cesspool of misery, of self-loathing. To hold you. To smile with you. To be there for you. To give you everything you ever wanted. To make a home. A life.

To make a family.

Aimee…

I'm so sorry I couldn't protect you. I'm so sorry I lied to you. Please forgive me. Please tell Isobel that I love her. That she's everything to me. Please tell her that I would never intentionally hurt either of you. Everything that I am I owe to you, Aimee. Everything that I was is dead because of you. I'm strong because of you. I'm happy because of you.

And I'm alive because of you.

Never forget that.

Never forget what you both mean to me. How much I love you both. How much I need you both.

There's nothing that I wouldn't do for you. Nothing that I wouldn't sacrifice to keep you safe.

Lucy is standing beside me. She's smiling; crying. She's telling me something. Can't make it out. Can't make out the words. But they're gentle words, words of love. They remind me of that first night we slept together. How sweet she was. How much fun she was. Before the bitterness consumed her. Before the pain, the loss, took hold of her. She takes my hand. It feels cold at first, but then somehow warm, even in the cold rain. I tell her that I'm sorry for everything. That I'm sorry I left her alone that night. Alone to die.

Don't know if she can hear me over the deafening noise. *It's getting closer.*

And closer, until the screaming train engine is all I hear.

Time freezes the moment I step onto the tracks. But it's long enough to hold Lucy near, to cradle her, whisper again for forgiveness. To let my family live in peace. Without fear. Without pain.

I think she hears me. I think she understands now.

I love you, Aimee. I love you more than words could express.

Keep Isobel safe.

Tell her that I'm sorry.

Tell her that I love her.

Tell her—

EPILOGUE

Standing in the bathroom doorway, I watch Aimee as she removes her makeup with a cleansing pad. Don't know why she bothers wearing the stuff; she looks better without it. Not that fussed on women plastered in foundation and eyeliner. It's not natural.

Although, natural or not, I'm glad she shaves her legs. Definitely not that fussed on the cave-girl look either.

Even though I've watched her a hundred times before, tonight, for some reason, seems different. Almost like the first night we spent together, or when we brought Isobel home from the hospital; every emotion turned up to eleven.

I'll always cherish those moments.

Just before I leave to check on Isobel, I catch a glimpse of Aimee's phone on the bedside table. I smile when I see her screensaver—it's another embarrassing photo of me, this time passed out drunk in Nia's birthday party.

Where the hell are all the nice pictures of me?

Tiptoeing across the landing, I gently prod Isobel's bedroom door open. She's sitting at the centre of her room, playing with her princess castle and dolls, locked in fantasy. She doesn't see me at first, so I sneak in, not wanting to spoil her playtime. I crouch down by her bed, smiling, watching from afar, wondering how on earth we made such a stunning, perfect daughter; so polite; so thoughtful; so beautiful.

I whisper that I love her. She doesn't hear me. This time I whisper her name. *Isobel, my darling.*

She still doesn't acknowledge me.

That's okay. She's probably too engrossed in another one of her princess adventures. She doesn't need me spoiling her fun. It's not that important. As long as I can watch.

As long as I can feel her warmth when she's near.

As long as I can hear her sweet voice when she laughs, when she sings.

And as long as I can watch her grow into the wonderful person I'm certain she'll become

I see you, Isobel.

I see you, Aimee.

I'm always here.

Always near.

Always watching...

FREE BOOKS

For a limited time, you can download FREE copies
of *Spine, Burn The Dead*, and *Rotten Bodies* -
The No.1 bestsellers from Steven Jenkins.

Just visit: www.steven-jenkins.com

ABOUT THE AUTHOR

Steven Jenkins was born in the small Welsh town of Llanelli, where he began writing stories at the age of eight, inspired by '80s horror movies and novels by *Richard Matheson*.

During Steven's teenage years, he became a great lover of writing dark and twisted poems—six of which gained him publications with *Poetry Now*, *Brownstone Books*, and *Strong Words*.

Over the next few years, as well as becoming a husband and father, Steven spent his free time writing short stories, achieving further publication with *Dark Moon Digest*. And in 2014 his debut novel, *Fourteen Days* was published by Barking Rain Press.

You can find out more about Steven Jenkins at his website:
www.steven-jenkins.com
www.facebook.com/stevenjenkinsauthor
twitter.com/Author_Jenkins

ALSO AVAILABLE

FOURTEEN DAYS

Workaholic developer Richard Gardener is laid up at home for two week's mandatory leave—doctor's orders. No stress. No computers. Just fourteen days of complete rest.

Bliss for most, but hell for Richard… in more ways than one. There's a darkness that lives inside Richard's home; a presence he never knew existed because he was seldom there alone.

Did he just imagine those footsteps? The smoke alarm shrieking?

The woman in his kitchen?

His wife thinks that he's just suffering from work withdrawal, but as the days crawl by in his solitary confinement, the terror seeping through the walls continues to escalate—threatening his health, his sanity, and his marriage.

When the inconceivable no longer seems quite so impossible, Richard struggles to come to terms with what is happening and find a way to banish the darkness—before he becomes an exile in his own home.

"Fourteen Days is the most purely enjoyable novel I've read in a very long time."

RICHARD BLANDFORD – The Writer's Workshop

Available at:

www.steven-jenkins.com

Amazon & all other book retailers

Burn the Dead: Quarantine

(Book One)

It's a dirty job - but someone's got to do it.

Robert Stephenson burns zombies for a living.

It's an occupation that pays the bills and plays tricks on the mind. Still, his life is routine until his four-year-old son becomes stranded in a quarantined zone, teeming with flesh-eating rotters.

Does Rob have what it takes to fight the undead and put his broken family back together?

Or will he also end up in the incinerator…

…Burning with the rest of the dead?

"If you're looking for a fast-paced zombie read, I highly recommend Burn the Dead by Steven Jenkins (5-STARS)"

K.C. FINN – Readers' Favorite

Available at:

www.steven-jenkins.com

Amazon & all other book retailers.

Burn the Dead: Purge

(Book Two)

There are those who run, while others hide.

And then, there are the Cleaners.

The living dead have staggered straight out of hell, and all that keeps humanity from crumbling is a small team of men who catch the rotters, before cleaning up the mess left behind.

Catherine Woods might not be a man, but no sexist, out-dated nonsense is going to stop her from following her dreams and joining the war against the undead.

The only problem is—even the best dreams can become nightmares in an instant.

"Filled with the perfect mix of crazy, jaw-snapping zombies, heart-stopping horror, Burn the Dead: Purge is a 5-star read for any zombie fan who is looking for something that isn't your typical rotter story."

A.J. LEAVENS – Author of Death's Twilight

Available at:

www.steven-jenkins.com

Amazon & all other book retailers

Burn the Dead: Riot

(Book Three)

A sold-out stadium.

A virus unleashed.

For 17-year-old Alfie Button, today was always going to be a memorable day.

The cheers of excited fans soon become desperate, bloodcurdling cries for help as a legion of the undead overwhelms the stadium. Panic erupts as 21,000 people rush for the exits, only to find them sealed.

With nowhere to run, suffocating in a torrent of blood and chaos, all Alfie and his friends can do is fight for survival—and pray that help will come.

But in every game, in every stadium…

There has to be a loser.

"I love the world the author has created—lots of action and real characterization."
JAMIE WHITE – Author of The Stains Trilogy

Available at:
www.steven-jenkins.com
Amazon & all other book retailers

THEA: A VAMPIRE STORY

(BOOK ONE)

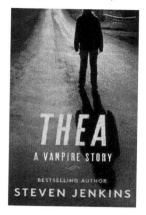

How far would you go to protect your child?

Vampires are real - hidden among us, concealing their lust for human blood. But monsters come in many forms. Teenage boys, drug addiction, underage sex - single mother Sarah battles to keep these demons from her daughters.

As the long nights of worry start to feed Sarah's paranoia, she must take desperate measures to save her family.

Although sometimes, the only way to kill a monster…

…is to become one.

"The epitome of chilling vampire noir. Cements Jenkins' pre-eminence in the realm of terror."

NATHAN JONES – Author of THE NOWHERE

Available at:

www.steven-jenkins.com

Amazon & all other book retailers

SPINE

Listen closely. A creak, almost too light to be heard…was it the shifting of an old house, or footsteps down the hallway? Breathe softly, and strain to hear through the silence. That breeze against your neck might be a draught, or an open window.

Slip into the pages of SPINE and you'll be persuaded to leave the lights on and door firmly bolted. From Steven Jenkins, bestselling author of *Fourteen Days* and *Burn the Dead*, this horror collection of eight stories go beyond the realm of terror to an entirely different kind of creepiness.

Beneath innocent appearances lurk twisted minds and scary monsters, from soft scratches behind the wall, to the paranoia of walking through a crowd and knowing that every single eye is locked on you. In this world, voices lure lost souls to the cliff's edge and illicit drugs offer glimpses of things few should see. Scientists tamper with the afterlife, and the strange happenings at a nursing home are not what they first seem.

So don't let that groan from the closet fool you—the monster is hiding right where you least expect it.

"If you love scary campfire stories of ghosts, demonology, and all things that go bump in the night, then you'll love this horror collection by author Steven Jenkins."

COLIN DAVIES – Director of BBC's BAFTA winning: The Coalhouse

Available at:

www.steven-jenkins.com

Amazon & all other book retailers

ROTTEN BODIES

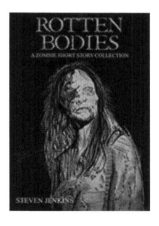

We all fear death's dark spectre, but in a zombie apocalypse, dying is a privilege reserved for the lucky few. There are worse things than a bullet to the brain—*much* worse.

The dead are walking, and they're hungry. Steven Jenkins, bestselling author of *Fourteen Days* and *Burn The Dead*, shares six zombie tales that are rotten for all the right reasons.

Meet Dave, a husband and father with a dirty secret, who quickly discovers that lies aren't only dangerous…they're deadly. Athlete Sarah once ran for glory, but when she finds herself alone on a country road with an injured knee, second place is as good as last. Working in a cremation facility, Rob likes to peek secretly at the faces of his inventory before they're turned to ash. When it comes to workplace health and sanity, however, some rules are better left unbroken. Howard, shovelling coal in the darkness of a Welsh coal mine, knows something's amiss when his colleagues begin to disappear. But it's when the lights come on that things get truly scary.

Six different takes on the undead, from the grotesque to the downright terrifying. But reader beware: as the groans get louder and the twitching starts, you'll be *dying* to reach the final page.

"Utterly hair-raising, in all its gory glory!"
CATE HOGAN – Author of One Summer

Available at:
www.steven-jenkins.com
Amazon & all other book retailers